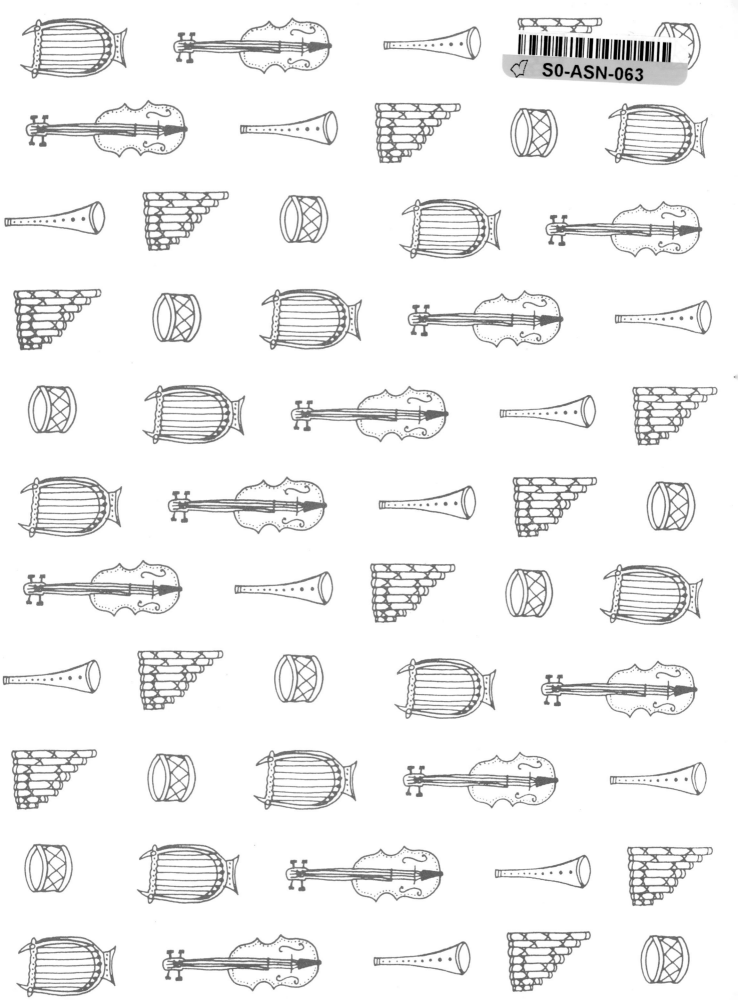

The Random House Book of

OPERA STORIES

For Francesca Dow and Laura Cecil

—A.G.

Text copyright © 1997 by Adèle Geras.
Illustrations copyright: *The Cunning Little Vixen* © 1997 by Ian Beck; *Aida* © 1997 by Louise Brierley;
Carmen © 1997 by Emma Chichester Clark; *Cinderella* © 1997 by Susan Field;
The Love for Three Oranges © 1997 by Katya Mikhailovsky; *Turandot* © 1997 by Sheila Moxley; *The Magic Flute* © 1997 by Jane Ray;
Hansel and Gretel © 1997 by Sophie Windham. Costume designs © 1997 by Rosemary Vercoe.
All rights reserved under International and Pan-American Copyright Conventions.
Published in the United States by Random House, Inc., New York.
Originally published in Great Britain as *The Orchard Book of Opera Stories*
by Orchard Books, a Watts Company, in 1997.
First American edition, 1998
http://www.randomhouse.com/

Library of Congress Cataloging-in-Publication Data: Geras, Adèle. [Orchard book of opera stories] The
Random House book of opera stories / retold by Adèle Geras ; illustrations by Ian Beck ... (et al.) ;
costume designs by Rosemary Vercoe. p. cm. Previously published: The Orchard book of opera
stories. Orchard Books. CONTENTS: The magic flute, or, The test of true love / music by Wolfgang
Amadeus Mozart ; illustrations by Jane Ray — Aida, or, Two lovelorn princesses / music by Giuseppe
Verdi ; illustrations by Louise Brierley — Carmen, or, The gypsy and the soldier / music by Georges
Bizet ; illustrations by Emma Chichester Clark — The cunning little vixen, or, Forest magic / music
by Leos Janácek ; illustrations by Ian Beck — Turandot, or, The ice maiden / music by Giacomo
Puccini ; illustrations by Sheila Moxley — Cinderella, or, The triumph of goodness / music by
Gioacchino Rossini ; illustrations by Susan Field — Hansel and Gretel, or, The defeat of the nibbling
witch / music by Engelbert Humperdinck ; illustrations by Sophie Windham — The love for three
oranges, or, A somewhat silly story! / music by Sergei Prokofiev ; illustrations by Katya Mikhailovsky.
ISBN 0-679-89315-6 (trade) — ISBN 0-679-99315-0 (lib. bdg.)
1. Operas—Stories, plots, etc.—Juvenile literature. [1. Operas—Stories, plots, etc.] I. Beck, Ian, ill.
II. Title. MT95.G47 1998 782.1'0269—dc21 97-51795

Printed in Dubai 10 9 8 7 6 5 4 3 2

The Random House Book of
OPERA STORIES

Retold by Adèle Geras

Illustrations by
Ian Beck
Louise Brierley
Emma Chichester Clark
Susan Field
Katya Mikhailovsky
Sheila Moxley
Jane Ray
Sophie Windham

Costume designs by Rosemary Vercoe

Random House ⌂ New York

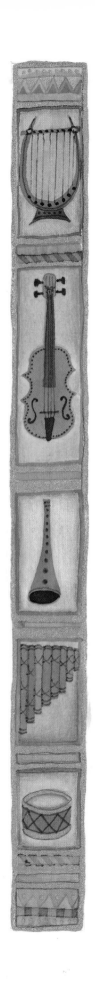

CONTENTS

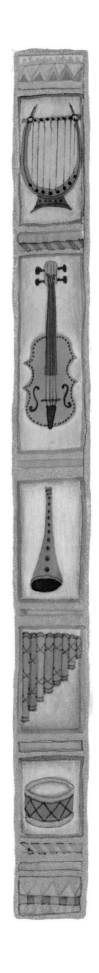

Wolfgang Amadeus Mozart
1756-91

By the time he was six, Mozart was giving concerts in royal palaces all over Europe. He is one of the very greatest of composers, and his music is loved throughout the world.

Mozart wrote The Magic Flute (*Die Zauberflöte*) in 1791, the year of his early death. He devised it with his friend Emanuel Schikaneder who took the role of Papageno (which perhaps explains why Papageno has so much to do!). Schikaneder was the director of a theatre company and very fond of magic and special effects. The opera is full of them. Mozart's own sister-in-law was the first Queen of the Night and Mozart himself once played Papageno's bells during a performance.

Though the story itself is rather eccentric, in the opera house The Magic Flute *is a most moving theatrical experience. A famous critic described it as the only opera in existence "that might conceivably have been composed by God".*

1756-
1791

Wolfgang
Amadeus
Mozart

THE MAGIC
FLUTE

The Test of True Love

The story I'm going to tell you is about so many strange and wonderful things that I fear you may become dizzy with the wonders of it. You will see dragons and angels, and visit temples and dungeons; old crones will change into beautiful young women, a young couple will walk through fire. You'll tremble before the Queen of the Night, and hear the melody of the magic flute, whose music weaves through the story like a silver thread. But for all its complications, this is a tale about two very different couples and how they each find True Love.

Let us begin with the Queen of the Night. She ruled the dark sky and wore the stars as jewels on her gown. No one dared to disobey her, for she was very powerful. She had three ladies who carried out her orders, and one day they looked down to earth and saw a prince running and running to escape the clutches of a ferocious, scaly dragon.

"Quick!" said the first lady. "We must save him! He is Prince Tamino." And the three ladies took their weapons and pierced the creature through the heart.

The dragon sank to the ground, stuck all over with silver spears, and the Prince stumbled and fell and lay quite still. The three ladies looked down at him.

"Oh, he's very handsome, isn't he?" said the first. "But the poor young man is stunned. We must tell the Queen about this at once."

"You two go," said the second lady, stroking Tamino's brow, "and I'll stay here and see that he comes to no harm."

"No, sister," said the third lady. "We will all go together."

And they vanished in an instant.

Suddenly the air was filled with the trilling, happy music of the pipes, and along came Papageno. He was bird-catcher to the Queen of the Night, and was hung about with cages. He was singing his favourite song: the one about what a fine bird-catcher he was.

"Oh, my fluttered feathers! What's been going on here?" he said, nearly tripping over Tamino's body. "Someone has had an accident, I see."

He put his cages down, and it was only then that he caught sight of the dragon's body. This gave him such a fright that he almost fainted.

feathered headdress

tattered frockcoat, covered with feathers

patched brocade waistcoat

striped patched trousers

PAPAGENO

"A dragon! Save me! Help me!" he cried. But then he noticed the silver spears. "Ooh, thank goodness for that," he sighed. "The creature's dead as a doornail. Panic over!"

Prince Tamino opened his eyes. First he saw the dead dragon, and then he saw Papageno, who said:

"No need to worry, dear sir. The dragon is dead, and I should know … I killed it myself. No need to thank me. It was nothing, really. Anyone would have done the same."

The three ladies appeared suddenly out of the blue air.

"You are a liar, Papageno," said the first, "and for this we will punish you."

She clamped Papageno's mouth shut with a metal padlock, so that he couldn't make a sound.

"You'll keep silent," she said, "or the Queen of the Night will hear of it."

Papageno trembled. As I've told you already, everyone was afraid of the Queen of the Night.

The ladies turned to Tamino.

"Prince, our mistress commanded us to save you, and she sends you this portrait of her daughter."

Tamino looked at the picture of a beautiful young woman, and at once his heart was filled with love for her.

"Her name is Pamina," said the second lady. "She's been imprisoned by an evil wizard. The Queen herself will tell you

more. Listen, she's coming."

The sky darkened, thunder rumbled in the distance, and all at once the Queen of the Night appeared, in a cloak made of night skies and starlight. Her grandeur and majesty filled Tamino with awe, but he could see that she was sad.

THE QUEEN OF THE NIGHT

indigo silk cloak

embroidered stars

pink brocade underskirt

pink satin slippers

"Hear me, Prince," she sighed, "and learn of my daughter's fate. A wicked enchanter called Sarastro has stolen her away and locked her up, and I cannot bear to be without her. If you will set her free, and bring her back to me, then you shall marry her."

Tamino said: "I'd do anything to win her. But tell me what I must do."

"My ladies will instruct you," said the Queen, and she rose up and up into the clouds and was gone.

"First of all," said the first lady, "this magic flute will help you whenever you need it."

A shining silver instrument appeared in the air above Tamino's head and glittered as it floated down into his hand.

"And of course Papageno will go with you," said the second lady, "to be your helper."

She removed the lock from the bird-catcher's mouth, and he began to speak immediately.

"Listen, dear ladies," he said, "rescuing princesses from evil wizards isn't my cup of tea at all. Bird-catching is all I'm fit for, honestly."

"The Queen has spoken," said the third lady, "and, besides, we'll give you this set of magic bells. Play them whenever you need help."

Papageno took the pretty silver bells, and played a tune that rippled and sparkled like a sunlit stream.

"Lovely!" he said. "Let's hope they can also keep us safe."

"Now, which is the way to Sarastro's castle?" asked Tamino. No one answered. The three ladies had vanished into the blue air.

In their place stood three young boys, who looked like angels.

"We'll show you the way, Tamino," said one. "We're spirits sent to help you at all times. You should go in that direction." He pointed his finger.

"Aren't you going to help me too?" Papageno asked, and one of the angelic boys answered: "Your way lies over there." And he pointed in the opposite direction.

So it was that Tamino and Papageno were separated, and Papageno found himself in Sarastro's castle.

"I'll try this door," he said to himself, and

suddenly he was in Princess Pamina's bedchamber. But who was the evil-looking creature leaning over the Princess as though to kiss her?

"My name," said this man, "is Monostatos, and Sarastro is my master. Princess Pamina is my prisoner, and I shall lock you in with her while I tell my master that you're here."

He strode out, and a heavy key turned in the lock.

"Don't be alarmed, Pamina," said Papageno as the Princess shrank from him in fear. "I'm not sure how I came to be here, but it's your mother's magical doing, I think. Prince Tamino has been chosen to rescue you. He's a brave and handsome prince and I'm his assistant. Papageno the bird-catcher at your service."

He sang a little tune and smiled at her.

"Oh, thank you, Papageno. That hideous Monostatos thinks that I'll agree to be his wife, but I never will. Never."

"Tamino loves you," said Papageno. "I only wish I could find a pretty young lady as well … Papageno seeks Papagena! I've been looking everywhere."

"I'm sure," said Pamina, "that you *will* find someone to love. You have a beautiful voice and you must have a kind heart because you've come here to rescue me."

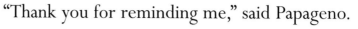

turban and make-up

TIGER

red slippers and gloves

"Thank you for reminding me," said Papageno. "We must get away. If we open the window we'll be able to step out on to the battlements. We mustn't be here when nasty old Monostatos returns."

Pamina and Papageno climbed out of the window and down a flight of steps leading to a courtyard. They had escaped, like two birds flying from a metal cage.

I hope you haven't forgotten about Prince Tamino. He had found his way to the gates of a magnificent temple. He tried to enter, but the gate was locked against him.

"What do you seek?" asked a priest. "This is the temple of Reason and Light."

"I've come to rescue the Princess Pamina from the clutches of the evil wizard Sarastro. Her mother, the Queen of the Night, has charged me with this task."

"You have been tricked," said the priest. "The evil one is the Queen herself, and Sarastro is great and holy. I can explain no more to you now, but you'll understand the truth very soon."

A great darkness then fell over the temple and the lands around it, and a voice spoke out of this darkness, and said: "Princess Pamina is alive. Do not lose courage."

Tamino put the magic flute to his lips and began to play an enchanted tune. Light filled the sky, and every living creature crept out of its hiding-place in rock or tree or sand and approached Tamino, bewitched by his melody. Then the trill of the bird-catcher's pipes came to them on the breeze.

"That's Papageno!" Tamino said. "He must be here somewhere." And he raced off in one direction to look for him, just as Pamina and Papageno appeared from the other direction.

"I heard the magic flute," said Papageno. "So Tamino must have been here."

They didn't see Monostatos creeping up behind them.

"The Prince has gone, but I've hidden here, waiting for you!" he hissed. Then he said to his slaves: "Seize them! Lock them up!"

BIG DOG

Papageno remembered his magic bells just in time. He began to sing:

"Silver bells, as I play. Take this horrid man away!"

The music was magical and cast a spell over Monostatos and his minions, who began to spin and twist, and twist and spin, dancing and turning slowly, moving further and further away from Papageno and Pamina, their legs carrying them far into the distance.

"That," said Papageno, "was what I call a narrow shave. We're safe at last! But, oh no, who can this be now?"

"It's Sarastro," said Pamina. "Isn't he grand and dignified?"

Sarastro strode from the temple in his robe of sunlit gold. His priests followed him in solemn procession.

"Pamina," he said, "my child, you must forgive me. Believe that I am your father and that I love you. I have only taken you prisoner to keep you from the evil influence of your mother, the Queen of the Night."

"I'm sorry I tried to escape, Father," said Pamina, "but Monostatos wants to marry me, and I couldn't bear the thought."

As though Pamina's voice had conjured him up, Monostatos himself arrived before Sarastro. At his side stood Tamino, who was now his prisoner.

When Pamina looked at the Prince, she knew at once that he was her rescuer, and her heart was filled with a great love for him.

"Princess Pamina," said Tamino, "you are even lovelier than your portrait."

"Sarastro," said Monostatos, "do I receive no reward for capturing this upstart prince?"

"On the contrary," said Sarastro, "I shall punish you for your wickedness. Take him."

The slaves led Monostatos away. Then Sarastro turned to Pamina and Tamino.

"What I am about to do," he said, "is for the best, even though it may seem cruel to you now. Tamino and Papageno, my priests will blindfold both of you and take you to the temple. There are three tests that you must pass. The first is Temptation, the second Fire and the third Water. They will be difficult, but if you succeed the reward will be very great."

Tamino and Papageno listened in silence as Sarastro told them about the first test.

"You must keep completely silent throughout all your trials. You must not speak, even if you are tempted by the kindest and gentlest of women. Then, when you have walked through fire and water, your reward will be Pamina's love and her hand in marriage."

Tamino agreed at once, but Papageno muttered:

"I'm not terribly good at shutting up. I don't think I'll ever be able to pass this test. As for being tempted by women, well, I'd enjoy it so much that I'm sure I'd never be able to resist … oh, dear, this isn't going to be easy!"

The three ladies floated out of the blue air as he spoke. Their voices lulled Papageno, and he was almost ready to be moved by what they said.

"Come back into the service of our Queen, dear Papageno," they whispered, and they stroked his hair and blew kisses at Tamino.

"Papageno, don't listen to them!" said Tamino sternly. "Remember – this is a test, and these are nothing but dreams sent to deceive us. Don't listen. And remember, whatever you do, keep silent!"

Far away from the temple, in her bedroom in the castle, Pamina was sleeping. She was dreaming of Tamino and did not know that Monostatos was leaning over her pillows, ready to kiss her. She awoke quite suddenly, and there was the Queen of the Night at her side. Monostatos quickly hid himself in the bed-curtains.

"Mother, what are you doing here?" Pamina said.

"I've come to give you this dagger," said the Queen, "and to beg you to kill Sarastro."

With these words she slipped like a shadow from the room.

"I heard that," said Monostatos. "I heard you planning to kill Sarastro. Say you will be mine for ever, or I'll go to your father and tell him what you and your mother are plotting."

"No," said Sarastro, who was suddenly beside Pamina. "Love and Friendship and Forgiveness rule in my temple, and I will not take vengeance on your mother, Pamina. Dry your tears. Monostatos, leave this room and do not return to trouble us."

He took Pamina in his arms and comforted her. "All will be well," he promised.

Let us return to Papageno. He was miserable. He hated silence and the gloomy dungeon in which he was imprisoned, and so he was playing his bells and singing to himself. He looked around suddenly and saw an old woman at his side.

"Have a drink, my dear," she said to him. "You look thirsty."

"I am," whispered Papageno, "but I'm not supposed to be speaking to you. Who are you?"

"Me? Don't you recognise me? I'm the love of your life."

Papageno roared with laughter. "You've certainly got a sense of humour, I'll say that. Love of my life indeed!"

He looked again at the old crone, but she had gone and in her place stood a lovely young woman, as plump as a partridge and dressed in a gown made of feathers.

"Oh my word!" said Papageno. "Whoever are you?"

"I'm Papagena," she said.

"What a coincidence," said Papageno. "I'm Papageno."

"I told you I was the love of your life, didn't I?"

"Did you?" said Papageno. "I thought that was someone else. How delightful you are! Marry me at once and we will live happily ever after."

"With pleasure," said Papagena. "We'll be as carefree as birds in a nest, together with all our pretty little chicks."

"Lots of little Papagenos!"

"And Papagenas!"

"Of course," said the bird-catcher, and he kissed his new love.

Two of Sarastro's priests came in and pulled them apart.

"Oh dear," said Papageno, "I'll never see you again. How sad. This is my punishment for speaking when I should have shut up. But where's Tamino? I can hear his flute, but I wish I could see him."

"Here he is," said one of the priests, "and here comes Pamina, too, summoned by his melody."

Papageno watched. Pamina ran to Tamino's side, but, of course, he could not speak to her. The three angelic boys were standing behind him.

"Why are you so cruel?" Pamina sobbed. "You do not love me any more. I shall use this dagger to end my life." She tried to plunge the knife into her heart, but Tamino's three heavenly helpers stepped forward and held her hand, so that she couldn't move at all.

"I'm also very unhappy," said Papageno. "I shall hang myself and put an end to my miserable life."

One of the guardian angels snatched away the rope Papageno had taken out of his pocket, and then, magically, Papagena was at his side again, and saying: "I've come back, you see, and now we shall always be together."

"How wonderful!" said Papageno. "But what about Tamino and Pamina? She thinks he no longer loves her, and he still has two more tests to undergo."

The priests said:

"The walk through Fire and the walk through Water are tests which you may face together."

Tamino and Pamina went down the stone staircase into the dungeon. All around them flames leapt and crackled. They held hands, and wherever they put their feet the fire shrank back like a living thing and was swallowed up by the shadows. When every spark had died away, they found themselves walking into a clear river which rose around their bodies and almost pulled them down into its green depths. They looked into one another's eyes and saw nothing of the water around them. Tamino played the magic flute, and its music lifted all their suffering away. They came out at last into the sunlight, in front of the temple. Sarastro was waiting there, ready to make them man and wife.

"What's that noise?" said Pamina.

"Nothing of any importance," said Sarastro. "Your mother and Monostatos are making an attack on the temple, but my priests will defeat them, never fear."

And that is indeed what happened. A joyful chorus rang out. Papageno and Papagena embraced in a fluttering of feathers, and Tamino and Pamina were led away to be married and to live for ever in perfect harmony and peace.

RACCOON

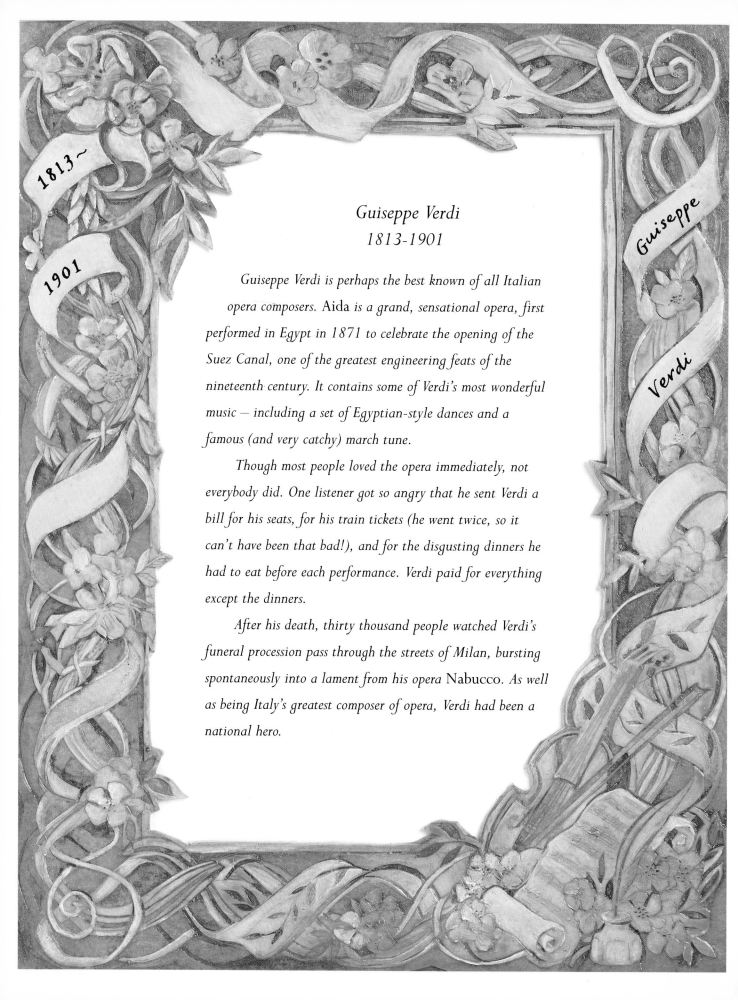

Guiseppe Verdi
1813-1901

Guiseppe Verdi is perhaps the best known of all Italian opera composers. Aida is a grand, sensational opera, first performed in Egypt in 1871 to celebrate the opening of the Suez Canal, one of the greatest engineering feats of the nineteenth century. It contains some of Verdi's most wonderful music — including a set of Egyptian-style dances and a famous (and very catchy) march tune.

Though most people loved the opera immediately, not everybody did. One listener got so angry that he sent Verdi a bill for his seats, for his train tickets (he went twice, so it can't have been that bad!), and for the disgusting dinners he had to eat before each performance. Verdi paid for everything except the dinners.

After his death, thirty thousand people watched Verdi's funeral procession pass through the streets of Milan, bursting spontaneously into a lament from his opera Nabucco. As well as being Italy's greatest composer of opera, Verdi had been a national hero.

Two Lovelorn Princesses

I am the Princess Amneris, and the King of Egypt's daughter. All my life I've lived in a splendid palace and been given everything a young woman could wish for. My handmaidens tend me from the moment I wake up, my clothes are made from the finest silks, and I have carved boxes full of jewels. But what use is all of that when I'm so miserable? I am in love with Radames, the Captain of my father's Guard, and oh, how I long for him to love me! There's no one here at court who can comfort me. It's Love that makes me cry, and keeps me awake at night. Radames is the husband I want.

We are at war with the Ethiopians, and yesterday Ramfis, the High Priest, came to Radames and said:

"You have been chosen to lead our troops into the next battle with our enemies."

He spoke as though this were a high honour, and I suppose it is. Men never think of how we, the women, will fret and sigh and imagine their bodies lying dead on the sand. I said nothing, even though I was in the room when Ramfis gave Radames this news, but what I was thinking was: Perhaps if Radames defeats our enemies and returns victorious, my father will order him to marry me.

There was a time when I thought he could grow to love me. We used to walk together in the evening, along the banks of the Nile, and my handmaidens would walk some way behind us, because of course they knew how much I wanted to be alone with Radames. It's almost impossible to hide things from the women who take care of me, but I have become better at it. Even my most devoted

AMNERIS
(Egyptian Princess)

handmaiden does not guess at my unhappiness every time I think of Aida! And who is Aida? you may ask.

She is an Ethiopian, captured after some battle or other, and my father gave her to me as a slave. She is graceful and well spoken, with a dignity you don't often find among ordinary people. She holds her head high, as though she has a right to look even the noblest Egyptian in the face. Everything she had to do she learned quickly, and she never seemed to show any resentment or bitterness. I was so friendly with her to begin with that it was easy to forget that she was born an enemy of our people.

I have left until last the most important thing about her, almost as though I don't wish to be reminded of it. Aida is beautiful. This wouldn't matter – some say I'm beautiful too – but Aida … well, she seems to have attracted Radames. Oh, it's so hard to bear!

Whenever she's with me in the room and Radames is there too, his eyes turn to her … they seem to linger on her face. She's also different in his presence. I've seen her bow her head so that she won't have to look at him, and she … well, she catches her breath when he speaks. I haven't said a word to her about it, but every time I see her I can feel myself filling up with jealousy. And … she's only a slave and I'm a princess. How can Radames prefer her to me?

Yesterday, there was a ceremony to hand the battle standard to Radames. Aida was there with the rest. I saw how she trembled to see him appointed Captain of the Guard: she can't bear to think of him risking his life in battle. She turned pale when everyone shouted: "Return victorious!" even though she, too, said the words. Later she was weeping, and I was the only one who noticed.

My name is Aida. Everyone here in the Egyptian court thinks I'm a slave, but I never forget that I'm really a princess. I'm proud to be an Ethiopian, and I long for my country.

When I first came here, I used to cry every night from homesickness, but now I just carry the pain around in my heart and try not to let anyone see it. I don't know how I walk and talk and go through my days without bursting into tears. There is only one thing that keeps me strong, and that is my love for Radames. How did I ever think that being captured by the Egyptians was the very worst thing that could happen to me? It isn't. It's far worse to carry this secret close to my heart, and to make sure that no one guesses that I'm a princess.

Only one person knows, and that is Radames. How could I keep such a thing from the man I love? And I do love him, and that is the second terrible burden I have to carry. How can I possibly love him? He is an enemy … maybe the chief enemy of my people. It is his duty to conquer the Ethiopians. I feel as though I'm betraying my people by loving him, and if I remain loyal to my country, then I'm being false to the man I love.

AIDA
(Ethiopian Slave)

When I heard them preparing for another battle, I could not bear it. Radames said:

"If I am victorious, Aida, I will be able to ask anything as a reward, and I shall ask to marry you. The King will not be able to say no."

Part of me longs for that, and I live for the day when I will be Radames' bride, but there are so many obstacles in our way that I cannot imagine such a thing ever happening.

And then there's Amneris. When I first came to Egypt, I was grateful for her kindness. Now she is my mistress and I am her slave, but even though she has power over me in almost every way, she can't control Love, and I know – all her ladies know – that she loves Radames too. She doesn't make any secret of it. I've overheard her giggling with her maidens, laughing about how handsome he is, and how well muscled, after all his battles!

She never laughs in this way when I'm there. She speaks to me less and less, and she's cold towards me. It's almost as if she's guessed that Radames and I love one another. Could she have seen us? Heard us speaking? Perhaps we should be more careful.

Yesterday I went with her to the ceremony and stood beside her as she handed Radames the royal standard to carry into battle. I found I could hardly breathe as the High Priest and the King all wished for victory, but of course, I had to join in the shouts of: "Return victorious!"

Do I want Radames to return victorious? Can I really wish for the defeat of my countrymen? Do I want their dead bodies to be covered by the sands of the desert? No. I cannot wish for that. Oh, all I can do is weep. For myself, for Radames, and for all who are marching into battle.

Come, Amneris, I say to myself over and over again. Is this a proper way for a princess to behave? I am being torn apart by my suspicions! I can't go on like this, and so now I've found a way of being certain, of making Aida confess her love for Radames. It came to me just now, while I was watching my maidens dancing. The battle's over. The Ethiopians are defeated and my beloved is marching to Thebes at this very moment for the victory parade. I am ready to meet him. I have spoken to my father, and he'll tell Radames the good news: we're to be married. So if I, Amneris,

will be his bride, what does it matter that Aida, a mere slave, loves him? Surely a princess of the royal blood is a more suitable wife for such a noble soldier? But I'll never rest until I know whether Aida loves Radames, or whether it is my love for him that has made me so jealous.

I know exactly what must be done.

How could Amneris have played such a trick on me? How could she? I will never forget what happened at the victory parade. It was so hot. The sun burned down on our heads. We all stood on the royal platform watching the soldiers march by. I, Aida, was there with all the other servants, and no one knew how sad I felt to see my people dragged through the streets as captives of the Egyptians. Everyone was cheering and shouting. The gold and treasures of my country were displayed in front of everyone on carts and wagons. Amneris was wearing a robe embroidered with gold threads and studded with turquoises and pearls. She wasn't smiling. That was because of me. Her trickery had started while we were still in her chamber.

She said to me, quite lightly:

"What a happy day this would be were it not for the death of our noble Captain, Radames."

How foolish I was not to suspect a trap! All I heard were the words. I burst into tears. I couldn't help myself. I sobbed, and covered my face with my hands, and nearly fainted.

Amneris said:

"Stop crying, Aida. Radames is alive."

Her voice was like a cold wind. She added:

"I see it all now. You love him. I thought you did, and now I know."

She leaned forward and hissed:

"It won't help you. All your love is as nothing. I am the Princess and my father the King has promised me that Radames will marry me. So your tears are in vain. Dry your eyes and come with me to the victory parade. I want you to see what happens with your own eyes. I want you to see Radames taking me by the hand and promising to be my husband. Follow me."

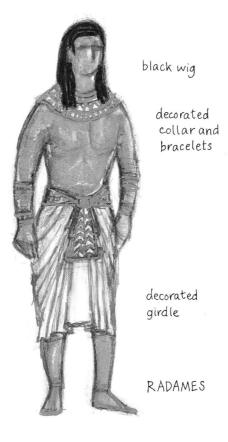

black wig

decorated collar and bracelets

decorated girdle

RADAMES

I thought: If only I could tell her! If only I could show her that I, too, am a princess, and just as suitable as she is to be Radames' wife! I was nearly weeping, thinking of this, when something even more terrible happened. I looked down at the Ethiopian captives and saw my own father, Amonasro, with his hands bound behind his back. What I did next nearly cost us both our lives. I ran to his side.

"Oh, oh, what have they done to you, Father?"

"Ssh, my daughter, do not say a word. The Egyptians don't know that I am the King of the Ethiopians. They will kill us both if they discover the truth. Keep silent."

I left my father and went to stand in front of the King.

"Sire," I said. "You have been so kind to me. This man is my father. I beg you, in the name of all your gods, set these captives free."

The High Priest, Ramfis, said:

"Do not listen, Sire. Kill all the Ethiopians."

"No," said Radames. "We are the victors and we can afford to be generous. We have their gold and their lands. Surely we may let them keep their lives."

"Let the others go, Sire," said Ramfis, "but keep Aida and her father as hostages in Egypt."

The King agreed.

"That is an excellent suggestion," he said.

Then he turned to Radames and I felt myself frozen into misery as he spoke:

"And to you, the victor, I give the greatest prize of all. I give you my daughter Amneris to be your bride."

Amneris had warned me, but nothing prepared me for how I would feel when I heard the words. Sorrow took hold of my heart and squeezed it until I found it difficult to breathe. I looked at Radames, and saw that he was pale. His eyes spoke to me of love, but my own eyes filled with tears and I could hardly see him. Oh, I don't know what is to become of us!

The banks of the Nile are beautiful, particularly at night. The reeds grow tall, and the stars seem very close in the blue velvet sky. The temple stands on the bank, and in the moonlight, its shadow falls over the water. Last night I arranged to meet Radames there for the last time. I knew that Amneris would be in the temple, making herself ready for her wedding.

"Poor Aida," she said to me. "I'm sure you will be happy one day."

She was right. I meant to put an end to my miserable life, and the only reason I had agreed to meet Radames beside the river was to say farewell to him. I was staring at the water, thinking of the cool darkness closing over my head for ever, when I heard a rustling in the reeds.

"Radames?" I whispered.

"No, it is Amonasro," said my father. "I must speak to you, daughter, before Radames comes."

"Hurry, then," I said. I couldn't bear to think of my very last meeting with the man I loved being spoiled. Still, my duty to my father meant that I had to listen to him.

"Daughter," he said, "the day is dawning when you will be a princess again. The Egyptians are preparing another attack on our soldiers, but we will be ready for them this time. If we can find out which way they will be marching, then we will ambush them, and they will be destroyed for ever. It all depends on you."

My father knew me well. He knew that I longed to see my country again, and he knew how my secret burned in my heart and would not let me rest.

"How can I help you, Father?"

"You must find out from Radames which way his army will march."

"But if he told me, he would be betraying his country. How can I ask him to do that?"

"If you don't, then I'll consider you a traitor. I shall hide behind this rock and listen to every word you say to him."

Then Radames arrived. What could I do? I begged him not to marry Amneris, to run away with me, and even as I asked him I knew he could not.

"You will be betraying your country and your king," I said. "I cannot ask that of you."

"We will go," he said. "We will take the same road as the army

when it attacks the Egyptians. We will go by the Napata Gorge."

My father sprang out from his hiding-place and told Radames exactly who he was. And he was not the only one who was listening to what Radames and I were saying. Amneris had left the temple some time before and she too had hidden and overheard our conversation. She summoned the priests and ordered them to arrest Radames. I had never seen her looking so angry. She said:

"You have betrayed me on the eve of our wedding, Radames, and it seems you have betrayed your country too."

Radames said:

"I will go with the priests and accept their punishment."

Then he turned to me and said:

"Aida, flee. Go with Amonasro before it is too late for you."

My father pulled me away and we ran together into the night. Radames, the soldier, the bravest man in Egypt, had tears in his eyes when he spoke to me.

What is the use of being the Princess Amneris when I cannot sleep for the sorrow in my heart? The conversation I had with Radames tonight has banished all my peace of mind.

When he came into my chamber, I had only one thing to say.

"If you could love me," I told him, "I will go to my father, and beg him to be merciful, and he will spare your life."

"You are very kind, Princess, but I have no wish to live. I cannot live without Aida, and they say that she and her father have been captured and killed."

"No," I said. "Aida is not dead. Amonasro was taken, but his daughter escaped, and no one knows where she is now. If you give up your love for her, I will save you. My love for you is as great as hers, I promise you."

"I could never love you, Amneris," Radames said quietly. "I will welcome Death like an old friend."

Those were his last words to me. I left the room, and the priests were summoned to take him away. He is to be entombed under the temple. He will never see the light of the sun again.

I am Aida, Princess of the Ethiopians, and I have found happiness at last. I hid myself in the underground chamber where I knew Radames would be locked up for ever.

"Beloved," I whispered in the darkness. "I am here. I have come to die with you. We will say goodbye to this world of misery and pain, and live together for ever in Paradise."

I am lying in Radames' arms, and I will never be unhappy again.

Radames must be dead. Who knows what has become of Aida? If I was unkind to her, I am sorry. Love is powerful, and we were both in its spell: two princesses who could have been friends, but were enemies instead. I'm crying for Radames. If Aida is dead, then I mourn her too. May the Gods help them to be happy in another world.

Georges Bizet
1838-75

Carmen *is Bizet's greatest work. Operatic myth has it that it was a complete disaster when it was first produced in Paris in 1875, but this is not altogether true. Some of the audience left before the opera ended, but* Carmen *went on to be a huge success when it was produced in other cities. Its melodies seem inexhaustible, and the use of Spanish rhythms and harmonies gives the opera a pungent, piquant flavour.*

Carmen *is perhaps the best-known and most popular of all operas, thanks to its skilful combination of a love story with passionate, lyrical music and, above all, a heroine who is a true free spirit. It is performed all over the world in every kind of venue. The tenor Caruso once sang the opera in an open-air bullring in Mexico during a rain-storm. When the opera was called off because of the rain the audience started rioting, so the cast had to continue. "We finisch the opera with a big pouring," wrote the wet singer to his wife afterwards, "and half of the public don't hear enytinks because the noise of the wather was strong on the umbrellas!"*

1838~

1875

Georges

Bizet

CARMEN

The Gypsy and the Soldier

My name does not matter, but remember the name Carmen, and listen while I tell you her story.

One day, long ago, a country girl called Micaela made a journey to visit her childhood sweetheart. His name was José, and he was a soldier. Micaela made her way to the main square of the town. There was a barracks on one side of this square, and a cigarette factory on the other. She spoke to Don Morales, the Captain of the Guard:

"I'm looking for Don José," she said. "I've walked all the way from his village, and I want to give him this letter from his mother. She misses him very much."

"He'll be here at noon, when we change the guard. You may see him then."

Micaela thanked the Captain, and went to find somewhere to rest while she waited for Don José.

Just then a whistle blew in the factory and all the young women who worked there came into the square to eat their midday meal beside the fountain. Carmen was among them.

How can I describe her to you, so that you understand the magic that she worked on every man who saw her? She was a Gypsy. She was beautiful, but others are beautiful, and they do not enchant men as she used to. They were all drawn to her. They looked into her eyes, and felt themselves pulled into depths they had not dreamed of. She loved passionately, it's true, but then another man would catch her eye and she'd lose interest. She reminded me of a soaring bird that would die sooner than be caged. And she liked to be the one who did the choosing.

"No man," she used to boast to her friends, "is going to pick me. Oh no! *I'll* decide who my love will be."

At last a small group of soldiers marched into the square to change the guard. You should have seen how they all fluttered around Carmen, flirting with her, trying to attract her attention, vying with one another to be the one, the lucky one, that she would choose!

"Why are you all making such an effort?" she laughed. "I'm much more likely to fall for you if you play hard to get! Don't you know that Love is like a naughty child? It's contrary. It'll do exactly what you're not expecting. You can never make Love do what you want."

Don José, Micaela's sweetheart, was one of the soldiers. He couldn't take his eyes off Carmen. At last she looked round and saw him. The whistle blew again.

"Come, Frasquita," Carmen said, turning to her friends, "and you, Mercedes. It's time to go back to work."

The women made their way to the factory, but Carmen went up to Don José. Taking the scarlet rose that was tucked into her hair, she threw it down at his feet and smiled. Don José gazed at her. His fate hung in the balance. I knew that if he stooped to pick it up, he was lost for ever, and his heart would be Carmen's to do with as she pleased. A silence stretched between them, and at last he bent down and picked up the rose. From that moment, he was bewitched, and could only follow the path that Destiny had marked out for him.

Soon afterwards, Micaela came back into the square, and although Don José was pleased to see her, and wanted news of his mother and his native village, half of him was somewhere else. After poor Micaela left, he hardly thought of her again. His head was full of visions of Carmen, and he still held the rose she had dropped.

All that happens is meant to happen: that is what the Gypsies say, and it was Fate that had a hand in what happened next. A fight broke out in the factory. No one knew what caused it, but that was not important. What mattered was this: Carmen had wounded another woman, and was arrested. Zuñiga, the Captain of Dragoons, put Don José in charge of the small party of soldiers that

was to take her to prison. Carmen smiled when she saw him.

"I saw the way you looked at me," she whispered, "and I know that we are fated to be together. Let me go free as we cross the bridge, and I'll meet you at Lilla Pastia's tavern. You will be my only love, I promise."

"How can I?" said Don José. "It is my duty to take you to prison."

"You can, because you are in my power," said Carmen. "You didn't have to pick up the rose, but you did, and it's a magic flower that binds you to me. Can't you feel it?"

I saw Don José protesting, but he was trapped by his love like an insect on a pin. What could he possibly do but let Carmen escape?

"Remember. Lilla Pastia's tavern," she murmured as she ran away, and Don José's head was filled with nothing but dreams of love.

Zuñiga was furious. "Fool!" he shouted. "You let the Gypsy escape and you must pay the price. I'll lock *you* in a cell, instead of her."

Everyone in the regiment knew that Zuñiga was himself attracted to Carmen, and Don José sighed to think how long it would be before he saw his beloved again.

sequined lace fan

tortoiseshell comb

CARMEN
(Bullfight
costume)

black slippers - laced

The months passed. One night, in Lilla Pastia's tavern, Carmen and her friends Frasquita and Mercedes were drinking wine and talking to the local smugglers, El Remendado and El Dancairo. Captain Zuñiga was there, too, pleading with Carmen for the hundredth time to forget about Don José and to love him instead.

"He's been locked away for so long," said Zuñiga, "that he's forgotten all about you. You say he'll come when he's released, but where is he? I know he left prison today."

"Then he will come." Carmen smiled at him and spun round on the dance floor, her skirts billowing around her. "I promised I would wait for him, and I never break my word."

"Listen!" Frasquita called. "I can hear something. It's Escamillo's procession, bringing him into Seville. Let's go and meet him."

Escamillo was a bullfighter, and in the days I am telling you of people would flock to see him wherever he went. How handsome he looked in his tight satin suit embroidered with sequins and jewels! How bravely he performed in the ring with the bulls every Sunday, and how swiftly and smoothly he slid his sword into the neck of every animal he faced! Escamillo greeted everyone, but his eyes fixed on Carmen.

"What is your name?" he asked her, and she told him: "Carmen."

"I will use your name," said Escamillo, "as a charm to keep me safe as I fight the bulls."

I recognised the way Carmen was looking at him. It was the look of a hungry child staring into the window of a baker's shop at a most delicious cake: no other cake will do – this is the one I want.

I trembled for Don José, for I could sense that Carmen was losing interest in him.

It was very late when Escamillo's procession left the tavern. Who can tell how things would have turned out if he had chosen to drink somewhere else that night? It is not for us to ask such questions.

"No sign of Don José," said Zuñiga to Carmen, "and now it is nearly morning. Come away with me."

"No!" shouted the smugglers. "Come with us and help to carry gold over the mountains."

Before Carmen had time to answer, Don José appeared at the door. His face was white.

"My Carmen," he cried. "You are here, just as you promised! I am yours, and bound to you for ever by a kind of spell."

Carmen and Don José danced together, and when the sun began to rise he sighed and said: "It's daylight. It is time for me to go back to the barracks."

"No," said Carmen. "Stay with me. Come and join the smugglers, and we will run away to the mountains and be free."

"I cannot desert my regiment," said Don José.

"And I," said Carmen, "can't love a coward who will not dare anything for me."

I think she was waiting for him to refuse her, for an excuse to leave and run into the arms of Escamillo, but it was not to be.

"Leave him," said Zuñiga from the other side of the room. "Why settle for a corporal when you could have a captain?"

Don José rushed at Zuñiga and tried to seize him by the throat, but the smugglers separated them and threw Zuñiga out of Lilla Pastia's tavern.

"Will you come with us?" Carmen asked Don José. "Will you stay with me?"

"I have no choice," Don José said. "I should have been at the barracks hours ago. I am already a deserter. You are my love and I will come with you."

So it was that Carmen and Don José joined the smugglers' band and went to live in the mountains.

A smuggler's life is hard, full of danger and with no great comfort. The lovers slept under the stars in the summer and in rough tents in the winter. They burned with love for one another at first, but in time Carmen became dissatisfied.

"Go home," she said to Don José. "Go back to your mother and your village and your childhood friend, whatever her name is. You are no smuggler. All you are good for is marching around in your silly uniform. Go!"

"I can't go," said Don José, "however much I may wish to. I love you now and I will love you for ever. I can never leave you."

"You love me now," said Carmen, "but if you stay, you will grow to hate me. You will probably kill me."

I knew that Carmen thought about Death all the time. Some

time before, she and Frasquita and Mercedes had dealt the cards, playing at fortune-tellers.

"I am looking for love," said Frasquita. "I want a young man to love me for ever."

"And I want an old one," said Mercedes, laughing. "A rich old man who will die and leave me all his money."

"Let me pick a card," said Carmen, and she took one from the pack and then another.

"Two of spades!" she cried, and said nothing else. We all knew that the two of spades could only mean Death, and that when the cards spoke, they spoke the truth.

"Death is walking towards me," said Carmen. "The cards never lie. Never."

So it was that Carmen knew a terrible fate awaited her, and that she was powerless to prevent it.

The next day the smugglers left Don José in charge of the camp and set off to take some contraband across the pass.

It was on this day that Micaela arrived, looking for Don José. She hid behind a rock before anyone saw her, because someone else had also arrived on the mountain. It was Escamillo, the bullfighter.

Don Jose began shooting at him.

"Stop!" called Escamillo. "I am not the police. I have come for Carmen."

"What if she will not come with you?" Don José asked.

"She will," said Escamillo. "She's been with a deserter from the army for months now, and I saw the way she looked at me."

"Don't you know," said Don José, "how dangerous it is to take a Gypsy's woman away from him?"

"You're no Gypsy," said Escamillo. "You're Carmen's soldier."

At that moment the smugglers returned. Carmen was with them.

"Go," said El Dancairo to the bullfighter, "before he kills you."

"I shall go," said Escamillo, "but I'm inviting all of you to the bullring on Sunday to see me fight. Those who love me" – he looked straight at Carmen as he said this – "are especially welcome."

As Escamillo went down the mountain the smuggler El Remendado found Micaela cowering behind a rock.

"I have come with a message for Don José," she said. "His mother is ill and wishes to see him. I beg you, Don José, come with me."

"Yes, go with her," said Carmen.

"And leave you free to go to Escamillo?"

Carmen pushed him away. "Yes! Our love is over. I wish you'd just go."

black braided hat

ESCAMILLO

gold braid, sequins and jewels

vermillion satin cloak

pink stockings

"We will meet again." Don José's voice was trembling as he left with Micaela. "I promise you that we will meet again."

The story could have ended there, with Don José returning to his home and his first love, and Carmen going to meet Escamillo in the town, but the cards never lie, and Death was in the cards.

A few Sundays later there was to be an important bullfight in Seville. Everyone put on their finest clothes and set off for the bullring, stepping out happily to the music of guitars and castanets.

I saw Escamillo arrive for the fight, and Carmen was on his arm. She had never looked more beautiful. She did not know that somewhere, in the crowds around the bullring, Don José was hiding, lying in wait for her. I had seen him, and so had Frasquita and Mercedes. They went to warn her.

"Carmen, he is here!" they told her. "Run away while you can."

Carmen shook her head. "I never run away. If Don José wants me, I will go and face him."

The bullfight had already begun when Carmen found Don José.

"My friends said you were here," she said. "They tell me you want to kill me."

"I have come," said Don José, "to beg you to love me once

more, because I cannot live without you. Forget the past and let's start again. I will do anything you ask."

"No," said Carmen, "I want to be free. I choose who I love, remember? And I no longer love you. Listen, they are clapping. The bullfight is over. I must go."

"You love Escamillo," said Don José. "Deny it if you dare."

"Why should I deny it?" Carmen laughed. "I admit it. I'm proud of it. Now let me go to him."

Don José threw himself at Carmen. "Either kill me," she hissed, "or let me pass at once."

She tore Don José's gold ring from her finger.

"There," she spat at him, "is the ring you gave me. I don't want anything of yours ever again."

Carmen's whole life had been moving towards this moment, the second when Don José took his knife out and stabbed her through the heart. She lay slumped in his arms, and he sobbed into her hair. He could have fled, but he stayed and let them find him.

"I've killed what I loved most in the whole world," he cried. "I don't care what happens to me. What is life worth to me without my Carmen?"

The police came for Don José and led him to prison. Carmen's stiffening body was taken away for burial. She is gone, but I have told you her story. Remember her. Remember how she loved her freedom, and how she followed her destiny, as we all must.

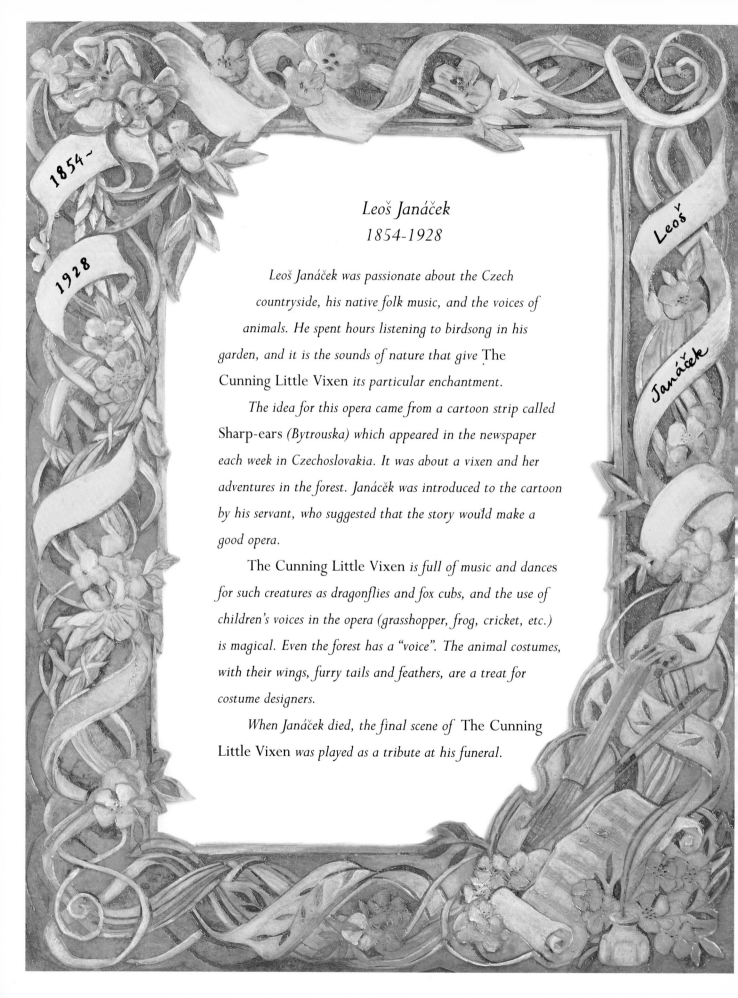

1854-

1928

Leoš

Janáček

Leoš Janáček
1854-1928

*Leoš Janáček was passionate about the Czech
countryside, his native folk music, and the voices of
animals. He spent hours listening to birdsong in his
garden, and it is the sounds of nature that give* The
Cunning Little Vixen *its particular enchantment.*

The idea for this opera came from a cartoon strip called
Sharp-ears (Bytrouska) *which appeared in the newspaper
each week in Czechoslovakia. It was about a vixen and her
adventures in the forest. Janáček was introduced to the cartoon
by his servant, who suggested that the story would make a
good opera.*

The Cunning Little Vixen *is full of music and dances
for such creatures as dragonflies and fox cubs, and the use of
children's voices in the opera (grasshopper, frog, cricket, etc.)
is magical. Even the forest has a "voice". The animal costumes,
with their wings, furry tails and feathers, are a treat for
costume designers.*

When Janáček died, the final scene of The Cunning
Little Vixen *was played as a tribute at his funeral.*

THE CUNNING
LITTLE VIXEN

Forest Magic

Listen to the rustling of the leaves! Every tree in this forest has a story to tell, and so have I. My tale is about Sharp-ears, the little vixen. My name is Owl, and I sit and watch the animals who live in the forest and the humans who come to it. I fly everywhere, and can see and hear everything.

The story began one summer day. The forest is at its most beautiful when the sun shines, and if you're lucky you may catch sight of the creatures who live there dancing and resting and dancing again. The dragonfly spreads her beautiful wings, the frog hops into the shadows and the badger dozes in the heat of the afternoon, brushing the flies away from his nose. Crickets sing, and their music fills the green spaces between the branches.

On such an afternoon a young vixen was enjoying her first summer, exploring the undergrowth and sniffing the earth. Then, when she saw a forester approaching, she hid herself among the ferns, for she knew that you had to be very careful of all humans.

"What a hot afternoon!" said the forester. "I'm going to lie down here in the shade and rest for a while, before going home."

wedding
headdress

velvet and fur-
trimmed cap

velour jacket
with braidings

SHARP-
EARS

The vixen watched as the forester closed his eyes, and then … what was that? A frog caught her eye. How tasty he looked! I knew that the vixen was going to chase him and eat him in one gulp. The poor frog hopped away.

"Help!" he cried.

One giant hop took him up and up – and he landed right in the middle of the sleeping forester's forehead.

The forester woke up as soon as the frog's cool feet touched his brow.

"What's that?" he cried, and made a grab to catch the creature. The frog slipped out of his fingers, and instead the forester caught the vixen by her tail.

"Oh ho!" he said. "You were after the frog as well, weren't you? Didn't look where you were going and now I've got you! What a beautiful creature you are! You remind me of someone I loved many years ago. She had red hair, just the colour of your fur, and her name was Terynka. I shall take you home to my wife and you can be a pet for the children. I shall call you Sharp-ears."

silk
bow

THE CUBS

57

The vixen spat and twisted, trying to get away, but the forester was very strong and he took her away to his cottage in a nearby clearing.

Sharp-ears was miserable.

"I wish I was back in the forest," I heard her say to the forester's dog. "I know that the man's wife gives us milk in a clean dish and feeds us well, but the children are forever teasing me, and now I'm tied up. Just because I tried to nip one of them."

"Well," said the dog, "you do sometimes nip them, and you always snarl at them, so I suppose you have only yourself to blame. Why don't you let me be your love? We could settle down together here, and lead a very pleasant life."

Sharp-ears thought the dog was boring and took no notice. She longed for the forest, and I think she was dreaming of finding a handsome fox to be her husband.

The forester's wife came out to feed the hens, and Sharp-ears watched as they scrabbled around for the corn.

"I don't think much," the vixen said to them, "of the life you have to lead! The rooster is your master, and all you can do is cluck and peck and obey him. You should spread your wings and fly away.

Be free!"

Sharp-ears was tied up, but the rope was long. The hens continued to cluck and peck, and this angered her. Finally, she could bear it no longer. She seized one of the birds and killed it, and after that she killed the others, one by one. Then, knowing she would be punished, she bit through the rope and ran away.

"Wait!" cried the forester, catching sight of Sharp-ears disappearing through the trees. "Come back to me!"

But the vixen did not return.

"I have lost her for ever," the forester sighed. "She was a free spirit, and couldn't bear to be tied up. Well, there's nothing to be done now but clear up the scene of the crime."

He began to pick the hens up by their feet. "My wife will moan about her birds," he thought, "but vixens were made to hunt and kill feathered creatures, and there's nothing we can do to change that."

I could see that Sharp-ears was happy to be back in the forest. She was sniffing the green grass and snuffling among the leaves, revelling in her freedom.

"Good day, young vixen," said the badger. "Where have you come from?"

"You don't recognise me, Badger," said Sharp-ears. "I was taken by the forester, do you remember? And now I'm back in the forest."

"Indeed, indeed," said the badger. "You have grown. Where are you planning to live?"

Sharp-ears ran round behind the badger and into the cosy sett he had dug for himself.

"I like it here in your house, Badger," she said, "so I advise you to find somewhere else. I have very sharp teeth, you know, and I won't hesitate to use them. Goodbye to you! You'd better hurry and find yourself a new home. I'm very comfortable here!"

She curled up and prepared to sleep. Settling down in the forest after so long among the humans was extremely tiring.

The days grew shorter and shorter as autumn turned the leaves of the forest to gold and bronze. The creatures who lived there closed their eyes and fell asleep. Then the winter came, and thick snow covered every branch, and drifted against the trees. Sharp-ears was snug in the badger's sett. The humans spent many winter evenings at the inn, drinking and talking about the days of their youth. The forester told his friends all about the pretty little vixen, and they teased him for not being able to keep her, once she had

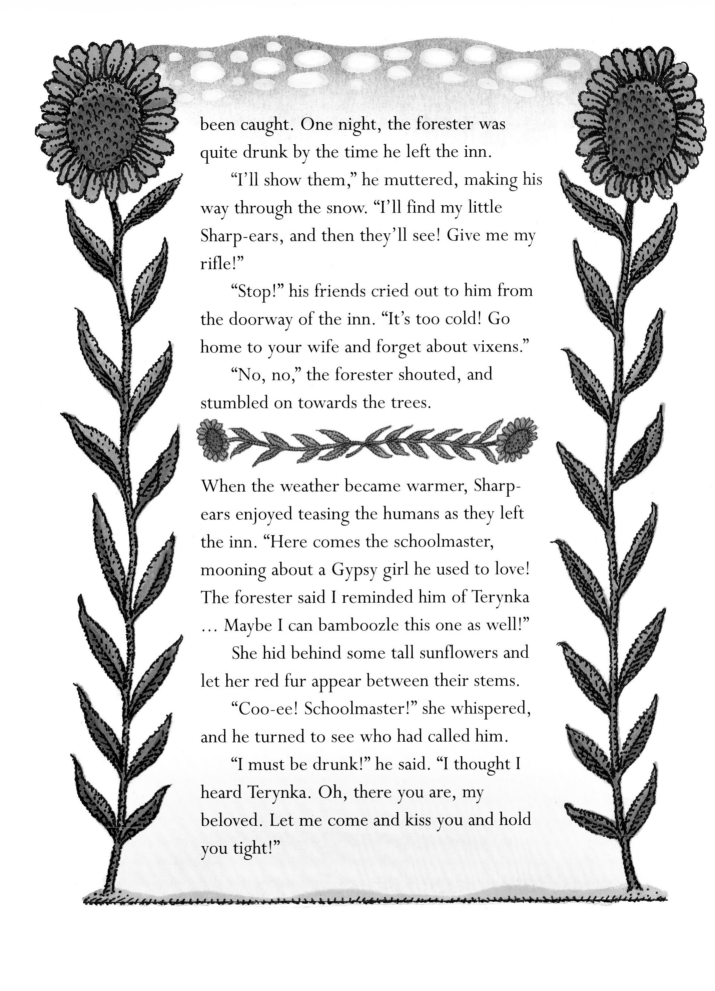

been caught. One night, the forester was quite drunk by the time he left the inn.

"I'll show them," he muttered, making his way through the snow. "I'll find my little Sharp-ears, and then they'll see! Give me my rifle!"

"Stop!" his friends cried out to him from the doorway of the inn. "It's too cold! Go home to your wife and forget about vixens."

"No, no," the forester shouted, and stumbled on towards the trees.

When the weather became warmer, Sharp-ears enjoyed teasing the humans as they left the inn. "Here comes the schoolmaster, mooning about a Gypsy girl he used to love! The forester said I reminded him of Terynka … Maybe I can bamboozle this one as well!"

She hid behind some tall sunflowers and let her red fur appear between their stems.

"Coo-ee! Schoolmaster!" she whispered, and he turned to see who had called him.

"I must be drunk!" he said. "I thought I heard Terynka. Oh, there you are, my beloved. Let me come and kiss you and hold you tight!"

fringed
woollen
shawl

HEN

He grabbed at what he thought was the shape of a woman, and was left clutching the sunflower plants.

"She's gone!" he wept. "She's left me again. I shall be alone all my life. How miserable I am!"

Sharp-ears laughed at him. "Silly humans! How easy it is to trick them!" she said.

She thought about teasing the priest as he went home, but I hooted a warning:

"Run away, Sharp-ears! Here comes the forester and he's got a rifle in his hand."

"I shan't let myself be caught twice," she said. "I'd rather be dead than be captured."

The vixen raced away and was lost in the darkness. The forester shouted:

"Sharp-ears! Where are you? I miss you! I'll find you, you'll see!"

But he did not find her, and gave up the chase and turned towards his cottage.

Then, one night when the moon was touching every tree with silver light, a handsome fox appeared in the forest. Sharp-ears saw him, and her heart was filled with love.

"Welcome to the forest," she said. "My name is Sharp-ears."

"I am Golden-mane," said the fox.

"And the name suits you," said Sharp-ears. "Come into my home, and we will see whether we are suited to one another."

"You are the most beautiful vixen I have ever seen," said Golden-mane, and he followed Sharp-ears happily.

dark
gloves

leather boots

GOLDEN-
MANE

The fox and the vixen stayed warm and hidden in their home all through the winter. In the spring Sharp-ears said to Golden-mane:

"How I love you, my darling Golden-mane! I always knew we were made for one another, and that's lucky, because very soon, we will be the parents of a litter of beautiful cubs."

"What wonderful news!" said Golden-mane. "We must be married at once and invite all the creatures of the forest to the wedding. I shall ask the woodpecker to perform the ceremony."

That was how the marriage of Sharp-ears and Golden-mane took place, and the creatures of the forest danced for joy. Every tree sang its own song, and the songs flowed together into a green melody that swelled and grew and rose into the sky.

I sat on my branch and watched the seasons pass. When the next spring arrived and the first new buds appeared, a litter of beautiful cubs was born to Sharp-ears and Golden-mane. The little foxes spent their days playing among the trees. By the time autumn came, the cubs were nearly grown.

The forester still walked among the trees, and one day, he found a dead hare. He said:

"I shall set this trap here for Sharp-ears. The dead hare is her work, I'm quite sure. I'll come back later, and maybe she will be caught after all this time."

The forester disappeared among the trees.

Sharp-ears, Golden-mane and their cubs came into the clearing.

"Look, Mama," cried the cubs. "Here's a trap! But we can see it, so we won't be caught. He's not a very good forester, is he?"

"Ssh!" said Sharp-ears, but she was too late. The forester, already on his way home, heard a rustling and a scuffling behind him.

"That might be a poacher," he muttered. "Or else it's Sharp-ears. I'll get her! I'll get her at last."

The young foxes watched the forester lift his rifle to his shoulder. A terrible noise split the silence of the forest, and then, suddenly, their mother was lying on the ground, still and lifeless.

"Run!" Golden-mane cried out to his cubs. "There is danger to

all of us if we do not hide at once."

The foxes fled back to their earth, to weep for Sharp-ears.

When the forester came to the clearing, he found her body lying on the ground.

"Oh, my cunning little vixen," he whispered. "At last you are mine!"

I watched and saw how sad the forester was, and all the forest creatures noticed with what tenderness he picked Sharp-ears up and carried her off. She lay heavy in his arms, and we could see his heart was full of sorrow. The birds crooned a mourning song, and the trees of the forest sighed with grief.

From my perch, I watched the forester lie down and sleep. All the humans had been to the inn, to celebrate a wedding. The forester had drunk a little too much beer. On the way back to his cottage, he began to feel drowsy.

"It's very warm," he said to himself. "I'll just lie down here for a while."

He slept. Perhaps he was dreaming of the vixen, Sharp-ears, and seeing her bright eyes and her fur the colour of flames. Then something woke him. He opened his eyes, and found a frog sitting on his hand.

"This is how it all began last time, little frog," he said. "This is exactly how I first saw her."

He looked up and saw a pretty fox cub, looking straight at him.

"You are very like your mother, little vixen," he said. "Run away into the forest. I'm going to rest now."

The forester lay down. Above his head, the dragonfly danced and the crickets sang their songs, and far, far above us all the wind blew through every tree in the forest, moving a million leaves into a rushing, rustling music.

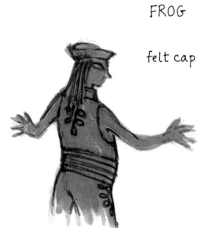

FROG

felt cap

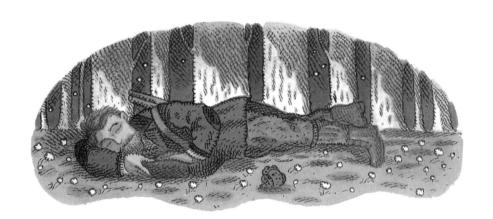

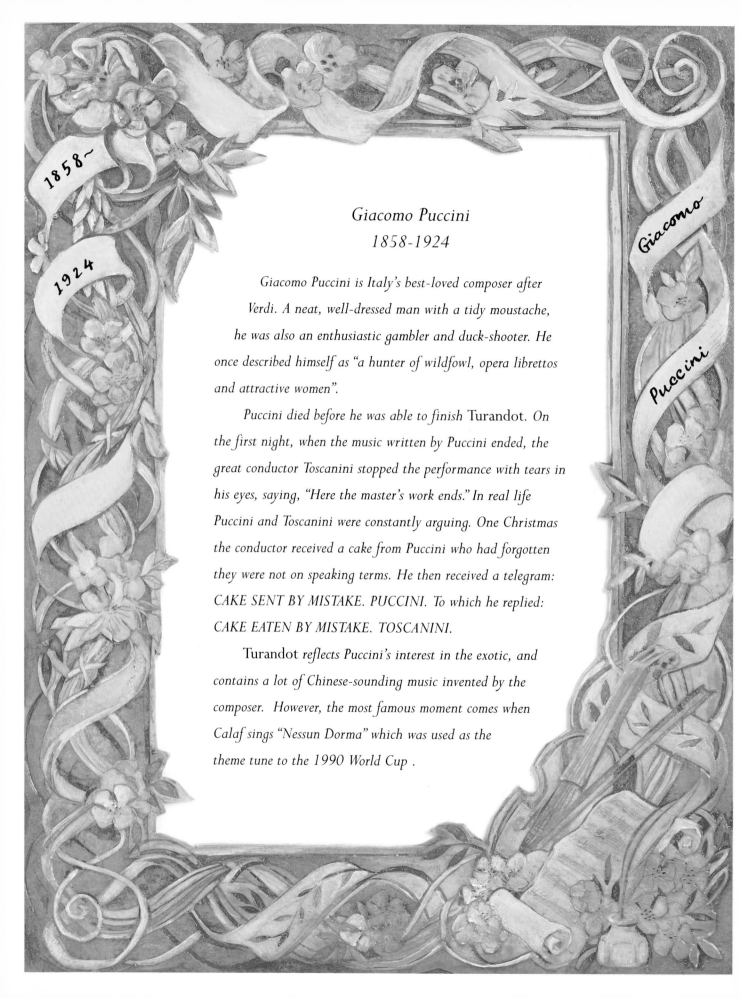

Giacomo Puccini
1858-1924

Giacomo Puccini is Italy's best-loved composer after Verdi. A neat, well-dressed man with a tidy moustache, he was also an enthusiastic gambler and duck-shooter. He once described himself as "a hunter of wildfowl, opera librettos and attractive women".

Puccini died before he was able to finish Turandot. *On the first night, when the music written by Puccini ended, the great conductor Toscanini stopped the performance with tears in his eyes, saying, "Here the master's work ends." In real life Puccini and Toscanini were constantly arguing. One Christmas the conductor received a cake from Puccini who had forgotten they were not on speaking terms. He then received a telegram: CAKE SENT BY MISTAKE. PUCCINI. To which he replied: CAKE EATEN BY MISTAKE. TOSCANINI.*

Turandot *reflects Puccini's interest in the exotic, and contains a lot of Chinese-sounding music invented by the composer. However, the most famous moment comes when Calaf sings "Nessun Dorma" which was used as the theme tune to the 1990 World Cup .*

TURANDOT

The Ice Maiden

When I was young, I had adventures, and now that I am old, all I can do is tell stories about them. My name is Calaf. I was born Prince of Tartary. My father, King Timur, had been banished from his lands after a war, and I had fled for my life and found myself in Peking.

I arrived in the city one evening at sunset. A crowd had gathered in the square in front of the Imperial Palace. I'd never before seen so many people together in one place.

"What's happening?" I asked, and someone said:

"Another suitor has failed to solve Princess Turandot's riddles, and will be executed as soon as the moon rises in the sky."

"Who is Princess Turandot?" I asked.

"She is the Emperor's daughter," said an old woman. "She's so beautiful that princes come from distant lands to ask for her hand in marriage, but she will have none of them. Her heart is carved from granite. She has announced that she will only marry the man who can solve three riddles she sets him, and those who fail … well, you can see what we are waiting for."

LIU

At that moment, a mandarin appeared and began to read from a scroll.

"People of Peking!" he cried. "The Prince of Persia has failed the test set by Princess Turandot, and will die when the moon rises."

Just then the guards began to push the crowds back, and I heard a woman cry out: "Look, they've thrown this poor blind man to the ground."

I stepped forward to help him, and as I lifted him to his feet I saw that he was none other than my own father, King Timur.

"Father!" I cried. "I've searched everywhere for you – and now here you are, and Liu, our faithful servant and friend, you are here as well."

My father said: "I couldn't have escaped without Liu's help. She's been my eyes when I needed to see, and someone to lean on when I was at my weakest."

"You're very kind, dear Liu," I said to her, "and I'm most grateful to you for looking after my father. But why should you make such a sacrifice?"

Liu looked down at her feet.

"Once," she said, "long ago in the palace, you smiled at me …"

She would have gone on and explained herself better, but a fanfare rang out, and she was interrupted. A procession came into the square, led by guards carrying an enormous whetstone on

which the executioner would sharpen his blade.

"Turn the whetstone!" the people shouted. "Let the moon rise in the sky like a white and severed head!"

I shivered, and said to my father:

"How bloodthirsty they all are! And what a terrible monster the Princess Turandot must be. Look, they are leading out the Prince of Persia."

The crowd fell silent when they saw him, suddenly saddened by the thought of his death. I looked up at the imperial balcony, and there was Princess Turandot herself, in a white robe that seemed fashioned from crystals of ice.

Her long black hair hung down her back and reached almost to her feet, and her face was a perfect mask, carved from whitest jade. Her lips, red as peonies, opened as she spoke, and ordered the executioner to proceed.

The poor Prince of Persia was led away to his death, but I, I'm ashamed to say, could think of nothing but the Princess. My heart filled with such love and such longing, just at the sight of her, that I could hardly breathe. When I found my voice, I made a vow. I made it aloud, so that everyone could hear me.

"I cannot live without the Princess Turandot as my bride. I shall solve her riddles and make her mine."

Liu began to cry.

"No, no," she sobbed. "You too will be beheaded, and I can't bear to think of it!"

"And I will lose you once again," my father said. "So short a time after finding you."

I didn't listen to them. I knew what I had to do. There was a huge brass gong in the square, suspended between two columns of lapis lazuli carved into the shapes of twisting dragons. Anyone who wished to present himself as a suitor to the Princess had to strike the gong three times. Rushing up to do just that, I found my way blocked by three elderly gentlemen dressed in the long robes of the imperial court.

"I am Ping, the Grand Chancellor," said the first man.

"I am Pang, the Marshal," said the second.

"And I am the Chief Cook," said the third. "My name is Pong. We have come to beg you to think again."

"Listen," said Pang. "Can't you hear the wailing of the phantoms that fly over the walls of this city? They are the ghosts of all who have loved Princess Turandot and died for love of her."

"She's only a woman," said Ping. "Surely you could love another woman just as much?"

"No," I said. "I could not."

I ran to the gong and struck it three times, my mind full of visions of the cruel maiden with the heart of ice and the lips like scarlet peonies.

No one thought that I could solve the riddles. Liu was crying. The three imperial gentlemen were muttering.

"When someone strikes the gong," Pang said, "Death smiles and makes ready to rejoice."

"We've seen so many deaths already," said Ping. "Six in the Year of the Mouse, and eight in the Year of the Dog."

"It's worse this year," said Pang. "We've had thirteen executions already. The city is awash with blood."

Nothing they could say would make me change my mind. I was more determined than I had ever been in my life.

Two guards led me inside the walls of the Imperial Palace. I stood in a vast square, with a marble staircase rising up from it and climbing as high as the Emperor's own chamber.

I watched as wise men appeared carrying scrolls which held the answers to the riddles. The ceremony was about to begin. The lantern-bearers carried both red and white lanterns: red for a wedding and white for a funeral.

At last, the Emperor Altoun took his place on the throne. He looked down at me and said:

"I beg you, my son, not to try and answer my daughter's riddles. I am bound by oath to let her ask them, but nothing

forces you to stay. Leave, before it is too late."

"Oh, Emperor and Son of Heaven," I said. "Let me try."

The Emperor asked me twice more, and I answered each time: "Let me try."

"Very well," he said. "Let the Princess approach."

Turandot appeared, and stood like a tall white candle beside her father's throne. Then she spoke, and I thought the heart would burst in my breast, so passionately did I love her.

"I am avenging the spirit of my ancestress, Princess Lou Ling," she said. "A thousand years ago, when dragons still flew among the mountain tops, a foreign king came to her in this place, ravished her and murdered her most horribly. To honour her memory, I have vowed never to let any man touch me. There are three riddles – there is only one Death."

"There are three riddles," I said, "but only one Life."

"This is the first riddle," said Turandot. "What is the phantom, born every night, which dies with the dawn, yet lives in human hearts?" I thought for some moments, and then answered: "Hope."

Turandot paused, and then asked the second riddle: "What warms like a flame, seethes in a fever, grows cold in death, but flares up at the thought of victory and glows like the setting sun?"

I answered: "Blood."

It was the right answer, and Turandot turned cold eyes

76

upon me. She was stiff with rage. But she continued.

"Answer me this then. What is the ice that sets you on fire? What consumes you, and yet freezes even harder?"

The crowd in the square stood silent and listened.

"Turandot," I said at last. "That is the answer. You are the ice which burns me."

The wise men nodded. This indeed was the correct answer, and Turandot flung herself sobbing at her father's feet.

"Do not force me to marry him," she cried, but the Emperor said:

"I have given my word, and marry him you must."

Turandot looked down at me where I stood and said:

"Surely you do not wish me to come to you unwillingly and trembling with fear?"

"No," I said. "I want you to be alight with all the fires of Love. If you can find out my name before dawn, I shall release you from your promise and die happily."

Turandot smiled, and her smile struck terror in the heart of everyone who saw it.

"Excellent!" she said. "I forbid the citizens of Peking to sleep until I learn your name. Tomorrow your neck will feel the executioner's sword."

That night the people of Peking stayed awake, unable to sleep. Their voices rose over the dark rooftops.

pearls, diamonds, crystal balls and drops

Turandot's headdress- front

ice-blue silk coat with embroidery, silver and pearls

TURANDOT

PANG
The Marshal

PING
The Grand
Chancellor

"No one is sleeping, but we will be no wiser in the morning."

I waited in the palace garden for the sun to rise. I thought: "No one is sleeping, but I am the only one who knows the secret of my name. When the sun rises, I shall be victorious, and then, Turandot, I shall be the one who tells you what it is."

Ping, Pang, and Pong came to me as I waited in the garden, and tried as hard as they could to change my mind. They offered me jewels and beautiful young women, but I refused all their gifts.

Then suddenly I heard shouting and loud cries. I ran to see

PONG
The Chief Cook

what was going on, and found guards dragging my father and Liu into the courtyard.

"These are the people who spoke to him," they said. "They surely know his name."

"No," I said. "They do not. This man and woman are complete strangers to me."

Turandot appeared just then and began questioning my father.

"Do not ask him, Princess," cried Liu. "He's nothing but a poor old man. I alone can tell you what the unknown Prince is called."

I tried to run to Liu's side, but the guards seized me. Turandot said:

"Hold him! Do not let him talk to her."

Someone in the crowd called out:

"Take the young woman. You can threaten her with such torments that she will tell you his name instantly."

"Never!" cried Liu. "I'll never tell it. I will die before it passes my lips."

I wept to see Liu's bravery and kindness, and even Turandot asked her:

"Why are you so brave? What has given you such strength?"

"Love gives me courage," Liu answered, "and even though your heart is still ringed with ice, by morning you will feel Love's power."

No one could have foretold what happened next.

Before anyone could stop her, Liu seized a dagger from one of the guards and plunged it into her breast. Then she stumbled to where I was standing and died at my feet. Poor, brave, loving Liu! She knew the fate that awaited her at the hands of the guards, and

chose her own death. For a moment I was so angry with Turandot I could hardly speak. Then I said:

"You are the Princess of Death."

"No," said Turandot. "I am the Daughter of Heaven and my spirit soars far above yours."

"Your spirit perhaps," I said, "but your body is here on the ground beside me."

I was too anguished to know what I was doing. I tore the veil from the Princess's face. I put my arms around her and my lips on hers. She fluttered in my grasp like a white bird, until at last the warmth of my love must have reached her and she began to weep.

"What's happening to me?" she whispered. "I've never cried in my life before."

"My love has warmed you," I said, "and your heart of ice is melting."

She looked into my eyes.

"I was afraid of my feelings for you from the start," she said. "Go now, and take the mystery of your name with you. I do not wish to know it."

"There is no mystery," I said. "I have won my victory and it no longer matters whether I live or die. My name is Calaf, Prince of Tartary."

Next day, the Emperor sat on his throne and Turandot and I stood beside him. The citizens of Peking had been summoned. Heralds trumpeted the news: the Princess had discovered the name of the unknown Prince, and an execution was certain.

"Tell me, daughter," said the Emperor with a heavy heart, "what is the name you have learned?"

Turandot smiled, and it was as though a waterlily had opened its petals for the first time.

"The name I have learned is Love," she said, and turned to embrace me.

The executioner sheathed his sword. It has not been needed here in Peking from the day Turandot promised to be my wife, and we have lived together happily for many years. Sometimes it is very pleasant to be old.

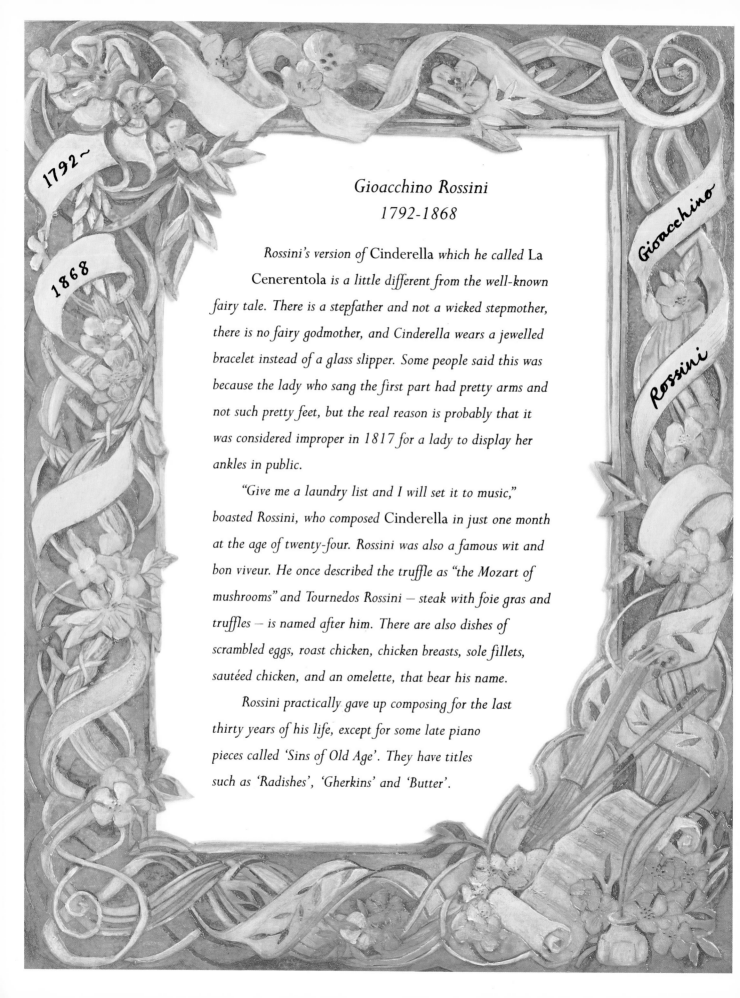

1792~

1868

Gioacchino

Rossini

Gioacchino Rossini
1792-1868

Rossini's version of Cinderella which he called La
Cenerentola is a little different from the well-known
fairy tale. There is a stepfather and not a wicked stepmother,
there is no fairy godmother, and Cinderella wears a jewelled
bracelet instead of a glass slipper. Some people said this was
because the lady who sang the first part had pretty arms and
not such pretty feet, but the real reason is probably that it
was considered improper in 1817 for a lady to display her
ankles in public.

"Give me a laundry list and I will set it to music,"
boasted Rossini, who composed Cinderella in just one month
at the age of twenty-four. Rossini was also a famous wit and
bon viveur. He once described the truffle as "the Mozart of
mushrooms" and Tournedos Rossini — steak with foie gras and
truffles — is named after him. There are also dishes of
scrambled eggs, roast chicken, chicken breasts, sole fillets,
sautéed chicken, and an omelette, that bear his name.

Rossini practically gave up composing for the last
thirty years of his life, except for some late piano
pieces called 'Sins of Old Age'. They have titles
such as 'Radishes', 'Gherkins' and 'Butter'.

CINDERELLA

The Triumph of Goodness

This story is about Cinderella, but it's a little different from what you are used to. It is, if you like, my version. My name is Alidoro. Ramiro is the Prince and his word is law, but, in a way, I am even more powerful. You could call me a kind of Fairy Godfather. For many years I was Ramiro's tutor, but I have other gifts. I can disguise myself so well that even my closest friends would not know me, and some say I am a kind of magician. This may or may not be true, but I do take some of the credit for the wedding we have just celebrated.

Of course, if Ramiro and his bride had not been attracted to one another from the very first moment they met, this would have been a different tale, but I'd always known that they were ideally suited, and so here is a story with a happy ending.

Everyone agreed that the Prince should find himself a bride. His dying father's last wish was that his son should marry as soon as possible, so all of us at court decided to hold a ball and to invite all the most beautiful ladies in the land.

I already knew that in the house of Don Magnifico there lived a

young woman whose name was Angelina, and who was as good as she was beautiful. Her widowed mother married Don Magnifico shortly after Angelina's birth. The couple then had two more daughters before the poor lady died. These young ladies were called Clorinda and Tisbe, and from their early childhood they had bullied, tormented and exploited their kind elder sister in every possible way, even changing her lovely name to Cenerentola, or "Cinderella", because she spent so much time sitting in the ashes of the hearth. Over the years, Don Magnifico had squandered all the money that his wife had left to her eldest daughter. Clorinda and Tisbe needed expensive, extravagant dresses and ridiculously trimmed hats for every new season, and their father's only hope of getting his greedy hands on some more money was to marry his daughters to rich men.

I went to Don Magnifico's house early one morning. I had put on a beggar's clothes. I could hear Cinderella's sweet voice singing as she made the morning coffee. She sang an old folk song about a king who found happiness by marrying a good woman and not a rich one. She was rudely interrupted. Even from the courtyard, I could hear Clorinda and Tisbe shouting at their poor sister:

"Come here, Cinderella, and help me to dress!"

"No, come to me first!"

"No, I insist!"

Backwards and forwards went their shrieks, on and on and on. I knocked at the door.

"Tell that beggar to go at once," said Clorinda.

"Yes," Tisbe added. "We are too busy to give alms. We are not even dressed."

They hurried away to their rooms, calling for Cinderella to come with them.

"I shall give you some food first," she whispered to me. "Sit here, sir."

"You are very kind," I said.

silk bonnets

CLORINDA and TISBE

I knew that the courtiers were on their way to the house to invite Don Magnifico's daughters to the ball, which was planned for that very night, and I looked forward to seeing what effect the invitation would have.

The courtiers arrived as I was eating. Clorinda and Tisbe came out to greet them. The invitation was issued and the young ladies began to flutter and squawk like two agitated chickens. They gave gold coins to the courtiers, but when they caught sight of me they were horrified.

"Go at once!" Clorinda said. "How can we possibly have beggars sitting about when we have to find suitable clothes in such a short time? The Prince might have given us a little more notice …"

"Come, Cinderella, we need your help even more now. I shall wake Father up and tell him the news. Oh, he'll be so excited."

"*I* shall wake him," said Clorinda. "I'm older than you."

"That doesn't matter a scrap," said Tisbe. "*I* shall wake him."

The bickering might have gone on for ever, but at that moment Don Magnifico woke up and bumbled downstairs in his nightcap.

"I've had the most extraordinary dream," he said. "The two of you were princesses, or queens."

Clorinda simpered. "Your dream could come true, Papa," she said. Then she told him about the ball, to be given so that Prince Ramiro could choose a bride.

muslin mob cap

CINDERELLA
(Kitchen costume)

shawl
(green-grey
wool)

"I am a prophet," said Don Magnifico. "Obviously, the royal bride will either be you, my dearest Clorinda, or you, my beloved Tisbe. Cinderella, bring me coffee at once! I must go and powder my best wig. Heavens above, what a to-do! Only a prince would dare to give a ball at such short notice."

I had laid my plans. The Prince and his valet, Dandini, were to exchange clothes so that Ramiro could see Cinderella without her guessing who he was. I also thought it would be amusing to see Clorinda and Tisbe flirting with a servant they had mistaken for a prince!

The kitchen was empty when Ramiro arrived. All I had told him was that someone most suitable lived in this house, and now he

TISBE

red satin
bodice
and
bows

was determined to come and judge for himself.

Cinderella came into the kitchen, singing her song under her breath. She stopped when she caught sight of Ramiro. He looked at her, and I knew that they were drawn to one another.

"Who are you?" Ramiro asked.

"I am Don Magnifico's stepdaughter," she answered. "I am a half-sister to Clorinda and Tisbe. I must go. The Prince's carriage will be here soon to take them to the ball."

Then Dandini arrived, prancing about in the grandest royal outfit he could find. The courtiers unrolled a carpet of red velvet which led from the carriage to the door, and he flounced along behind two footmen, enjoying the masquerade enormously. Don Magnifico greeted him in the most exaggerated manner, bowing so low that he almost fell over. He introduced Dandini to Clorinda and Tisbe, who were decked in more ribbons and ruffles, frills and feathers than you could find in twenty drapers' shops.

"What a treasure!" said Dandini, kissing Clorinda's hand. "And here's another." He kissed Tisbe in the same way. "How will I ever decide? My court tells me to hurry and find a bride, but what can I do in the face of such beauty?"

jewelled head-
band with roses
and lace

CLORINDA

Clorinda and Tisbe blushed and tittered. Don Magnifico was beside himself with delight. Cinderella approached her stepfather.

"May I come to the ball too?" she asked him.

"Certainly not," said Don Magnifico. "Go back to the kitchen."

"Come, sir," said Dandini. "Why can't this young lady join the festivities?"

"It wouldn't be suitable," said Don Magnifico. "She is nothing but a lowly servant."

I was by now no longer a beggar, but had disguised myself as a member of the Prince's court. I held an enormous book bound in leather, and I went up to Don Magnifico.

"In this volume," I told him, "are written the names of everyone in the kingdom. It appears that you, sir, have three daughters. So where is the third?"

CLORINDA and TISBE
(full view)

Of course I knew the truth, but I was curious to see what Don Magnifico's answer would be.

He began to sniff, and to wipe away false tears from his eyes.

"Gone," he sighed. "The angels have taken her to be one of their number. She is dead, alas and alack."

"But, Papa – " began Cinderella.

"Hold your tongue," Don Magnifico hissed at her, "or I shall punish you most severely."

Cinderella made her way sadly to her room. Clorinda and Tisbe and Don Magnifico leapt into the waiting carriage and were off to the palace with Dandini, leaving the courtiers to roll the red carpet up again.

When all was quiet, I came into the house again. I didn't want Cinderella to recognise me. After all, she had seen me twice today already, and so this time I dressed as a pilgrim and pulled my hood well over my face.

"Don't cry, Cinderella," I told her. "I've prepared a carriage for you, and a dress that befits your beauty. You *shall* go to the ball."

While I was transforming Cinderella, Clorinda and Tisbe and Don Magnifico were being entertained in the palace by Dandini. Don Magnifico had been led at once to the wine cellar.

"I have appointed you Royal Butler in charge of all my wines," said Dandini, and left Don Magnifico tasting the contents of one bottle after another, dictating orders to the courtiers, and growing more and more tipsy.

Dandini and Ramiro met in the royal gardens to discuss what

Dandini had discovered about Clorinda and Tisbe.

"They are vain and stupid young women," said Dandini, "and not worthy of Your Highness."

"I have found the woman I love," Ramiro told him.

"Ssh," said Dandini. "Here come Clorinda and Tisbe. Good evening, fair ladies. Let me present my manservant. I feel that you should meet him. I can only marry one of you, so perhaps the other could marry him. He's a fine fellow, I do assure you!"

"Marry a servant?" said Clorinda. "Never in my life! Look how common he is!"

"I agree with my sister," said Tisbe. "I could never marry such a vulgar creature. I'm far too refined."

Meanwhile I had come into the garden with Cinderella.

"I should like to present this young lady to you all," I said. "She wishes her name to be kept secret."

Cinderella lifted the veil, and her loveliness shone like the light of the moon coming out from behind a cloud.

Clorinda and Tisbe stepped back in amazement. "She resembles ..."

"It can't be ..." they murmured, both recognising and not recognising their half-sister. "No, no, we must be mistaken. Cinderella is at home."

I also noticed Ramiro staring at Cinderella. Who was this enchanting lady who looked so much like his beloved?

"Come," said Dandini. "Let us eat now, and I shall make my decision after dinner."

I could see that he, too, was bewitched by the unknown lady.

After dinner was over, it was clear that Don Magnifico was feeling a little conscience-stricken over his treatment of Cinderella, but Clorinda and Tisbe reassured him.

"The Prince is delighted with us," they said. "One of us is sure to be the royal bride."

In another part of the palace, the unknown lady was being courted by Dandini.

"I cannot be your bride, sir," she said, "for I love another."

Prince Ramiro stepped forward, still disguised as a manservant, of course.

"I beg you to marry me, madam," he said, and bowed. Cinderella recognised her beloved at once.

"If you can find my house," she said to him, "you will

learn the truth about me. Take this bracelet, and when we meet again I shall be wearing one just like it."

With these words, she turned and left the room.

"I swear that I will find her," Ramiro said, "and marry her as soon as possible."

A happy ending was easy to arrange. I wanted Don Magnifico to realise that he had been tricked, and that Dandini was really the Prince's servant. So next day a carriage carrying

Dandini – now dressed in his usual servant's clothes – just happened to break down outside Don Magnifico's house. He, naturally, was appalled.

"I am ruined!" he cried. "Oh, the disgrace, the humiliation!"

Clorinda and Tisbe, discovering they had been tricked, broke into howls of rage. Matters had been bad enough the night before when they returned from the ball to discover that it was indeed their half-sister who had dazzled everyone with her beauty, but this was too much! They had both been eager to marry a mere valet.

Then a terrible storm split the sky. Some say I called it up myself, but I don't pretend to have such powers. It just happened that the Prince's carriage was passing Don Magnifico's house, and so

Ramiro went in to take shelter. Cinderella was amazed to see that the person she had thought of as a manservant was none other than the Prince. He caught sight of the bracelet she was wearing almost at once.

"Dear lady," he said, taking its twin from his own breast pocket, "here is the bracelet you gave me. Come with me to the palace and we will be married tomorrow."

Horror, consternation and astonishment made everyone talk at once. I told Clorinda and Tisbe that everything they owned would have to be sold. Don Magnifico had spent the money Cinderella's mother had left her, and he would have to pay it back. The only way the family could avoid poverty was to beg forgiveness from Cinderella herself.

At first Clorinda and Tisbe would have none of this, but I persuaded them in the end. At the wedding they presented themselves before the royal couple, dressed soberly in plain clothes.

"Forgive us, dear sister," they said.

"Forgive me too," said Don Magnifico.

And Cinderella forgave them, because she was so kind. The words of the song she always sang had come true, and the Prince had chosen a wife for her goodness, which, as I often say, always triumphs in the end.

Engelbert Humperdinck
1854-1921

During the 1970s and 1980s, a pop singer whose real name was Gerry Dorsey called himself Engelbert Humperdinck and made many hit records. He took his name from the first Engelbert Humperdinck who was a brilliant music student and acted for a while as assistant to the famous composer Richard Wagner.

The première of Hansel and Gretel *was in 1893, conducted by another great German composer, Richard Strauss. The opera, which is the only work of Humperdinck to be staged regularly, began as a piece for children to perform at home, and is full of delicate, original music that makes use of native German folk song. The parts of both Hansel and Gretel are played by women. Everyone knows the famous fairy tale, but the opera has several characters (the Sandman, the Dew Fairy, the Angels and so on) who do not appear in the story.*

Hansel and Gretel *was the first complete opera to be broadcast on radio on 6 January 1923, from Covent Garden in London.*

HANSEL
AND
GRETEL

The Defeat of the Nibbling Witch

The forest was silent and green, but in its heart, hidden amongst its tallest trees, lived the Nibbling Witch. Everyone knew that she lured innocent children to her house, and baked them into honey cakes or gingerbread and nibbled them bit by bit. Children were warned to keep well away.

A broom-maker called Peter had built a small cottage at the edge of the forest. He lived there with his wife, Gertrude, and their two children, Hansel and Gretel. The family was poor and often there was no food at all on the table at supper-time.

One day, Hansel and Gretel were sitting and waiting, whiling away the time until their parents returned.

"When will they come?" Hansel wanted to know. "I do hope they bring some food. Do you think Mother's found mushrooms for supper? I'm so hungry."

Gretel had begun to darn some socks. "You're always hungry, Hansel," she said, but she went to the cupboard, and opened it.

"Here's a jug of milk for tonight, at least," she said, and she put it carefully on the table.

"Let me have one little sip now, sister," said Hansel. "Only one, I promise." He dipped his finger into the jug and licked the cream from it. "It's delicious."

"Certainly not," said Gretel. "Leave the milk alone, and I'll teach you a dance."

By the time their mother returned, Hansel knew the dance as well as his sister.

Gertrude was tired.

"You've done none of the things I asked you to do!" she said, and sank into a chair. Her skirt caught the handle of the milk jug and it fell to the floor. Every drop of milk in it was spilt.

"Oh!" Gertrude wailed. "Look what you've made me do! Our best jug is smashed to pieces, and there's nothing for supper. You children must go at once and find something for us to eat. Go a little way into the forest … not too far, now … or down to the river, and pick whatever berries or nuts you can find, or we shall all starve to death. Quickly, quickly! Take this basket with you."

Hansel and Gretel left the cottage, and before long Gertrude, nearly weeping with exhaustion and hunger, heard her husband singing as he came home from the market.

"He's been to the tavern," she thought, "and drunk a few beers before coming home, for he sounds like a happy man."

She prepared herself to shout. How dare he spend what little money they had on drink?

"Hello, hello, my dearest wife," sang Peter, coming into the cottage. "Look what I've got! Oh, it's many years since I've had such a successful market-day."

He opened his knapsack and took out of it all the good things that Gertrude and the children had been dreaming of: eggs, golden loaves of bread, small round potatoes, bunches of carrots and fat brown sausages bursting out of their skins. Gertrude stared at the food.

"Where are the children?" asked Peter. "Call them to see all this. They will be so happy."

"I've sent them out to pick some strawberries," said Gertrude.

"Where did you tell them to go?" cried Peter.

"To the forest," said Gertrude.

The joy left Peter's face. Furious and terrified, he shouted at his wife:

"Foolish woman! How could you do such a thing? The Nibbling Witch lives in the forest! We must go and look for the children at once. Let us pray that we are not too late."

Hansel and Gretel were resting in a clearing.

"Look how many strawberries we've picked," said Hansel. "At least we will have something for supper."

Gretel was sitting on a cushion of moss, making a garland of flowers to put in her hair. Hansel took a strawberry out of the basket and ate it. His sister frowned at him.

"I was just trying one," he told Gretel, "to see how sweet and juicy they are. Here, you have one. No one will miss two strawberries out of a whole basketful."

"Very well," said Gretel, "but only one." She ate the strawberry.

"Oh, how delicious!" she said. "Let's just have one more each, and then take the rest home."

One more each became two, and two turned to three, and then, before they knew it, there were no strawberries left at all.

"Oh, Hansel, what have we done?" cried Gretel. "Mother will be so angry."

"We couldn't help it," said Hansel. "We were hungry. I don't think I've ever been so hungry in my life. Let's go home and tell her we couldn't find any strawberries. The sun is setting and it'll soon be dark."

honeysuckle wreath

GRETEL

pink shoes

Hansel looked around him. None of the paths seemed familiar, so which one should he choose? Gretel followed her brother. The sun was going down and a shadowy twilight fell on the trees. Branches like twig hands clutched at the children's clothes. Roots hidden in the earth made them trip and stumble as they groped through the darkness, further and further into the green heart of the forest.

Suddenly the children stopped. What was that? They peered around the trunk of a tree and saw something magical hovering between the branches. It was a shape that shimmered and glowed, looking almost like a person, but blurred around the edges and surrounded by pale light.

feather in cap

necklace of string and feathers

HANSEL

old grey boots

"I am the Sandman," said this creature, "and the Bringer of Dreams."

As he spoke, he threw handfuls of glittering gold-dust into the air. The leaves of every tree were covered with it, and glittered in the dusk. Some of the dream-sand flew into the children's eyes and made them sleepier than they had ever been. They lay down.

"We mustn't forget our prayers," said Gretel.

The children knelt and said:

> "While we are sleeping
> Here on the ground,
> Come, guardian angels,
> And stand all around."

That night, Hansel and Gretel dreamed the same dream, in which fourteen angels floated above them, with their shining wings outspread to keep all harm away.

Just before dawn, the Dew Fairy, floating above the forest, came down and stroked the trees and the grass with her pale green fingers, leaving silver drops of moisture on everything she touched. Gretel woke up as the sun rose, and caught a glimpse of her.

"Wake up, Hansel," she said. "I've just seen the Dew Fairy

sprinkling us all over. She was so beautiful! Her skirts were made from mist, and her hair was like a waterfall. Wake up! Let's try and find our way home now. Imagine how worried Mother and Father must be."

Hansel stretched and yawned.

"I'm hungrier than ever," he said. "Maybe we'll find some berries as we go."

The children walked and walked, then Hansel said:

"Look at that cottage. Maybe whoever lives there will give us some breakfast and show us how to get home."

The closer they came to the cottage, the stranger it seemed. The fence was made of gingerbread men, standing all in a row. When they reached the door, Hansel said:

"This windowsill is made of cake."

"And the roof is tiled with biscuits," said Gretel. "The walls are covered in marzipan, and the door is made of chocolate."

Hansel broke off a corner of the windowsill and began to eat it greedily. A thin voice started singing inside the house:

"I can hear a little mouse,

Gnawing, nibbling at my house!"

"Who's that?" Gretel asked, and at once the chocolate door swung open and an old lady came out. She was dressed in a long black dress and a frilly bonnet, but her hands were like claws and she was holding an enormous butterfly net. Gretel called out, but Hansel was still eating, and the next moment the old lady had caught him in the net and was pulling him into the cottage.

"Wait!" Gretel shouted. "Where are you taking my brother? I'm coming too."

The inside of the cottage was very different from the outside. All the good things to eat had vanished and Gretel found herself in a huge, cavernous and echoing room. It was empty except for a metal cage and a gigantic brick oven. The old lady took off her frilly bonnet and her greasy hair tumbled and twisted down on to her shoulders like a coil of writhing black snakes.

"You must have heard of me," she said. "I am the Nibbling Witch. Your brother looks a tasty morsel. I shall put a spell on him and lock him in this cage until I am ready to bake him."

She began to chant:

> "Little boys
> Taste delicious.
> Boys are juicy
> And nutritious."

Gretel watched as the Nibbling Witch pushed Hansel into the cage, then picked up a branch of elder wood and hissed:

"Elder tree
Lock him tight.
Bind his limbs
Day and night."

Hansel became stiff all over.

The Nibbling Witch, delighted with her catch, jumped on to her broomstick and began to fly around the room, shrieking and cackling. Then she went to prepare the oven. Gretel seized the branch of elder wood and at once ran to the cage, saying:

"Elder tree
Set him free.
Work your charms,
Unlock his arms!"

Immediately, Hansel was released from the witch's spell.

"Her eyes are very weak," Gretel whispered. "She hasn't even locked the cage."

The Nibbling Witch then came back to inspect Hansel. She reached through the bars to squeeze his arm and see how plump he was, but Hansel put a stick into her hand and she felt that instead.

"You'll have to wait, my duck," she said, "for me to fatten you up, and meanwhile you" – she turned to Gretel – "go and see whether the cakes I am preparing are ready yet."

"Certainly," said Gretel, and she went to the oven and opened it. "The cakes *are* ready," she said, "but you must show me how to take them out."

"How stupid you are!" said the Nibbling Witch. "Why do I have to do everything myself?"

Gretel signalled to her brother, and as the hag made her way to the oven Hansel opened the door of his cage and crept up behind her. Then, when she bent in towards the flames, brother and sister pushed and pushed as hard as they could, and she fell into the fire. The screams of the Nibbling Witch were lost in the roaring and crackling of the flames. Hansel and Gretel shut the oven door behind her and Hansel said:

"Quick! We must escape, and we will take as much of this house as we can carry."

He began to break off pieces of the doorstep to put into his pockets. Gretel said:

"Hansel, look at the fence!"

Hansel looked. The fence made out of gingerbread men seemed to be crumbling. As the hard, brown biscuit fell away, Gretel said:

"Oh, there's a child baked into each one."

The children stood there with their eyes closed, until Gretel picked up the Nibbling Witch's branch of elder wood, saying:

"Elder tree,
Set them free.
Work your charms,
Unlock their arms."

huge
butterfly
net

pleated
bonnet

The children blinked and stirred.

"We're awake," they cried. "We're alive. Where's the Nibbling Witch?"

"She will not worry us again," said Hansel.

From behind the children came a rumbling and a thundering roar and, as Hansel and Gretel turned to look, the cottage swelled up with flames and exploded into the sky.

"Look what's fallen over there," cried one of the gingerbread children. "It's the Nibbling Witch. She's nothing but a honey cake now."

Hansel and Gretel's parents had been searching for them for many hours. Then, when they had nearly given up hope of finding their children, they heard the sound of happy voices and came running into the clearing.

"Oh, my darlings," said Peter. "Here you are at last! We have been searching for you all night long."

"Thank God we have found you!" cried Gertrude.

Hansel and Gretel hugged their mother and father, the gingerbread children gathered round, and everyone sang a hymn of praise. Hansel looked up at the sky and remembered his dream.

"There are our guardian angels, Gretel," he said. "Can you see them?"

"Yes," said Gretel and smiled at her brother. "They are always with us."

The fourteen angels smiled, their shining wings outspread to keep all harm away.

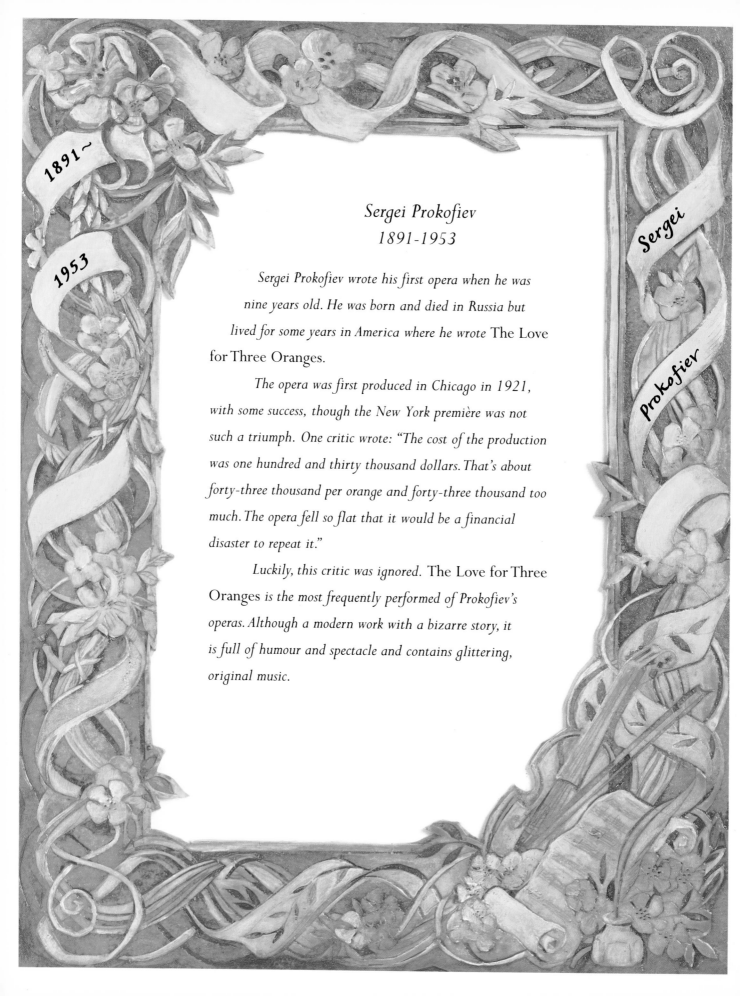

Sergei Prokofiev
1891-1953

Sergei Prokofiev wrote his first opera when he was nine years old. He was born and died in Russia but lived for some years in America where he wrote The Love for Three Oranges.

The opera was first produced in Chicago in 1921, with some success, though the New York première was not such a triumph. One critic wrote: "The cost of the production was one hundred and thirty thousand dollars. That's about forty-three thousand per orange and forty-three thousand too much. The opera fell so flat that it would be a financial disaster to repeat it."

Luckily, this critic was ignored. The Love for Three Oranges *is the most frequently performed of Prokofiev's operas. Although a modern work with a bizarre story, it is full of humour and spectacle and contains glittering, original music.*

A Somewhat Silly Story!

"Hurry! Hurry! Come and see the latest play! Can you hear the trumpets and the drums?" said Pantaloon.

Everyone in town was in the square. Whenever the players came to perform, the crowds gathered to look at the acrobats and the dancers, the jugglers, and the actors, like Pantaloon, in their strange masks and satin cloaks.

"Greetings!" shouted Pantaloon. "You are all waiting to see the show, and we have a wonderful surprise for you today, believe me."

"Let's have a good, weepy tragedy," someone shouted, and all his friends joined in:

"Yes, yes, give us tears and heartbreak. We love a good tragedy."

"No, no," came a cry from the other side of the square. "Side-splitting comedy is what we like! Give us a belly-laugh! Let's have banana skins for people to slip on, and custard pies galore."

"We want romance," some other voices cried. "We want love,

kisses, hard-hearted parents and thrilling elopements!"

"You will have something different today," said Pantaloon. "It is an unusual story called 'The Love for Three Oranges'."

"Whoever heard of such a thing?" said someone in the crowd. "Who could love three oranges? This is really most peculiar."

"We love strange stories," said a group of young men near the front of the stage. "The more eccentric the better."

"Then you will enjoy this performance," said Pantaloon. "The oranges are magic oranges, naturally. Now, pray silence for the actors and let the story unfold. Please transport yourselves to an imaginary kingdom, ruled by a great king. Here he is."

Everyone clapped as the King made his entrance.

"Oh, woe is me! That's my poor son, the Prince, over there. Look at him," said the King.

The audience turned to gaze at a white-faced youth, slumped gloomily in a chair.

"He is in a terrible state," said the King. "He suffers from every illness that you can possibly think of …" He began to walk up and down, listing ailments on his fingers. "He's got asthma, corns, rheumatism, arthritis, chilblains, headache, earache, palpitations, blurred vision, and those are only the illnesses I can pronounce."

"He should see the doctor," said Pantaloon.

"He sees a dozen prodding doctors every day," said the King. "Look, here they are now."

A dozen doctors were indeed prodding the poor Prince. They looked in his ears, they shone lights down his throat, they listened to his heartbeat, and they shook their heads.

"There's nothing we can do for him," said the dozen prodding doctors at last. "He's an incurable melancholic. He'd feel much better at once if only he could laugh."

"Oh, my son never laughs," said the King. "In fact, I can't remember the last time I saw him smile."

"We should try and make him laugh," said Pantaloon. "It's his only hope."

"Summon Truffaldino, my jester," said the King, "and let's see if he can devise some festivities that might amuse the Prince." He clapped his hands. "Truffaldino!" he called.

"Here I am, Sire," said Truffaldino. "At your service."

"Please, ladies and gentlemen," said Pantaloon, "clap whenever you see the jester Truffaldino. It encourages him."

The audience clapped. Pantaloon said:

"Now for something completely different. This side of the stage will become the infernal regions, and – look who's here! Let me introduce Fata Morgana, the witch. She's a baddie, so feel free to hiss whenever you see her."

Loud hisses filled the square. Pantaloon continued:

"She's playing cards, as you can see, with Good Wizard Chelio."

"Two of clubs," said Good Wizard Chelio.

"Eight of diamonds," said Bad Witch Fata Morgana.

"Knave of hearts!"

"Queen of spades!" said Fata Morgana. "I've won! I've won and you've lost, and now the melancholy Prince is in my power. Come to the palace. There are goings-on there I wish to see."

At the palace, the pompous Prime Minister Leandro was plotting with the King's nasty niece Clarissa.

"They're baddies too," Pantaloon told the crowd, "so you're allowed to hiss at them as well!"

Everyone in the square hissed so loudly that Leandro and Clarissa had to wait some moments before they spoke.

"If the Prince is ill and never laughs," said Nasty Niece, "then he will not be a suitable king, and I will inherit the throne. You may marry me, Leandro, and together we will rule over everything."

"Excellent," said Pompous Prime Minister. "The Prince is most unlikely to laugh, so our plan should succeed very well."

"Psst!" said a voice, and then again: "Psst!"

"Who's that?" asked Clarissa the nasty niece.

"It's me, Smeraldina. I'm behind the curtain."

Clarissa pulled back the curtain, and there was a young maidservant.

"Ladies and gentlemen," said Pantaloon, "you'd better not hiss for Smeraldina. She's only a sort of assistant baddie. She's got a message for Pompous Prime Minister and Nasty Niece. Let's hear what it is."

Smeraldina said:

"I've just been to the infernal regions and Fata Morgana was playing cards with Wizard Chelio. She won, of course, but the Wizard's magic protects the Prince, and Truffaldino *is* very funny. If the Prince laughs, then he will become King and we will be his subjects."

"He won't," said Pompous Prime Minister. "But let us go and watch the fun."

Everyone trooped off the stage.

Pantaloon clapped his hands.

"Silence everyone! Here comes a new scene. We're in the throne room, and everyone's trying to make the Prince laugh. They're not having much success, are they?"

Pantaloon was right. The Prince sat flopped in his chair like a rather lumpy ghost.

When Pompous Prime Minister, Nasty Niece and Smeraldina

came in, the crowd hissed loudly at them. Then Fata Morgana and Wizard Chelio entered.

"Boo!" and "Shoo!" shouted the audience, so loudly that Fata Morgana slipped and tripped and her skirts flew up over her head. She was wearing purple knickers with huge pink and yellow spots all over them, and of course the whole audience roared with laughter. And – miracle of miracles – so did the Prince!

"Look!" said Truffaldino. "His Royal Highness is laughing!"

The Prince was indeed laughing, and so hard that he had to bend over to catch his breath, and then he had to ask Truffaldino for a hankie to wipe all the tears of laughter from his eyes.

"Oh, my word," he said. "Those are undoubtedly the most hilarious knickers in the universe."

"How dare you call my knickers hilarious, young man?" growled Fata Morgana. "I shall put a curse on you, and that will teach you a lesson, so there! You'll fall in love with three oranges. You'll go to the ends of the earth to search for them, and when you find them, you may only eat them near water, otherwise terrible things will befall you.

Beware!" She clapped her hands. "Farfallo! Come here!"

An ugly little creature waddled up to her carrying an enormous pair of bellows.

"Who's this?" someone called out.

"Let me introduce Farfallo the devil," said Pantaloon. "Fata Morgana will tell you what he's come here to do."

"Farfallo," said Fata Morgana, "has come to blow the Prince and Jester Truffaldino to where the three oranges are to be found."

"Come on then, Truffaldino," said the Prince. "Let's go. That silly little devil is puffing us in this direction. If I must search for three oranges, then I'd like to get on with it."

Farfallo blew the Prince and Truffaldino right off the stage. Everyone clapped loudly and shouted:

"Change the scenery quickly! Let us see where the Prince has gone."

"A yellow backcloth," Pantaloon said to the audience, "means we are in the desert. And here comes Good Wizard Chelio, whose job it is to protect the Prince. Are you all following the action?"

"Greetings," said Wizard Chelio. "Where are we?"

"We're near the castle," said Silly Devil Farfallo, "where the three oranges are."

"That's that, then," said Wizard Chelio. "Let them fetch the fruit and we can all go home."

"Not so fast!" said Farfallo. "The oranges are guarded by

Creonte, the crazy cook."

"Crazy cook?" said Wizard Chelio. "Fata Morgana never said a word about a crazy cook. But do we have to worry about a mere cook?"

Farfallo chuckled. "This is not a mere cook. This is a fearsome, terrifying, giant crazy cook, taller than the tallest tower, broader than three elephants, and with teeth sharper than any saw. It goes without saying that he's very fond of the three oranges. Our heroes will be minced and ground up before you can say 'meatballs'."

The audience gasped when they heard this, and some of the smaller children hid their faces in their mothers' skirts. Whatever would a crazy cook look like?

"Hmm," said Good Wizard Chelio. "I haven't got many of my spells with me today, so this'll have to do, I suppose."

He went over to where the Prince and Jester Truffaldino were sitting in the shade of a rock.

"Your Highness," said Wizard Chelio, "here's a bunch of ribbons on a stick. There's a bell in there somewhere too. If you wave it at this crazy cook chappie, it might distract him for a moment, and you'll have time to steal the oranges and run away."

"Thank you," said the Prince.

"Come on," said Truffaldino. "Let's get into the castle. I'd like this adventure to be over."

Pantaloon appeared and bowed to the crowd.

"We're going to have a change of scene here." He clapped his hands. Two young men pushed a piece of scenery with a kitchen painted on it on to the stage. Then the monstrous Crazy Cook walked on. He was huge, and looked so frightening that many of the ladies in the audience nearly fainted.

"Don't be scared," said Pantaloon. "He's really three acrobats covered with a painted cloth."

On the floor in front of the Crazy Cook were three oranges, each one brighter and more juicy-looking than the next.

"Look, Mother!" a child called out. "There are the magic oranges."

"Grr!" growled the Crazy Cook. "What are you doing in my kitchen? I've a good mind to slice you thinly and fry you with onions."

"No, kind sir, please don't do that," said Truffaldino. "We've only come to bring you a gift. Look."

He waved the ribbon-stick and the little bell tinkled most musically.

"Oh, how delightful!" said the Crazy Cook. "How kind you are! It's just what I've always wanted. Give it to me."

While Truffaldino was handing over the gift, the Prince was pushing the oranges into his pockets.

"Quick, Truffaldino," he said, "let's get back to the desert. Then we can take these oranges and go home."

They ran as fast as they could, out of the castle.

"Ladies and gentlemen," said Pantaloon, "the kitchen scenery has

been removed. Please note the yellow backdrop. We are once more in the desert. It's noon and the sun is blazing down. The oranges, as you can see, have grown."

This was true. The oranges were so big that Truffaldino and the Prince could hardly push them across the stage.

"I'm exhausted," said the Prince. "I shall have a nap in the shade of this orange, and we'll continue when I've rested."

He lay down and fell asleep at once.

"It's all very well for him," said Truffaldino, "but I'm dying of thirst. I feel as if I'm burning up. And there's no water anywhere."

His gaze fell on the oranges. He smiled and winked at the audience.

"Look at this fruit, though! Isn't it the juiciest-looking thing you've ever seen? I shall peel this orange and eat it, and all will be well."

Pantaloon winked at the audience from the side of the stage and whispered:

"Oh dear, he's forgotten the warning! No oranges to be eaten except near some water!"

Truffaldino touched the orange. There was a flash and a bang. The peel fell away, and hidden in the fruit was a beautiful princess, who stepped out and said to Truffaldino:

"Good day, sir. I am Princess Linetta. I am extremely thirsty. Have you any water about your person? If you haven't, then I'm afraid I'm going to die instantly."

"Alas, madam, water is quite absent from this desert."

"Then goodbye," said Princess Linetta, and sank down dead at Truffaldino's feet.

"Oh dear," he said. "How very unfortunate! And I didn't get a single drop of juice from that orange. Perhaps I'll have better luck with the next one."

The second orange also had a princess hidden within it.

"My name," she told Truffaldino, "is Princess Nicoletta, and if I do not have a drink, I shall die instantly."

"Well," said Truffaldino, "I seem to be having a few problems with water."

Before he had finished his sentence, Princess Nicoletta lay dead on the sand.

"This is too much," sobbed Truffaldino. "I'm leaving. I cannot bear it."

He ran off the stage.

"Well now," said Pantaloon, stepping over the bodies of the Princesses, "what a calamity! Two dead Princesses. Hardly the sort of thing you see every day, is it?"

At that moment the Prince woke up.

"Ah!" he said. "I feel much better now ... but what's this? Two dead Princesses? What on earth has been going on? There's an awful lot of peel lying around, and only one orange left. I'm going to eat it. Why shouldn't I?"

The third orange opened up as soon as the Prince touched it,

and out stepped a ravishingly beautiful young woman.

"I am Princess Ninetta," she said.

"How lovely you are!" said the Prince. "I find myself quite passionately in love with you. Will you marry me?"

"I love you very much," said Princess Ninetta, "and I certainly will marry you if I don't die first. I need water. I need it at once."

"Of course!" said the Prince. "Fata Morgana warned me not to eat the oranges unless I was near water. Help! Truffaldino, where are you?"

The Prince raced away to find help, and suddenly the front of the stage was full of young men throwing buckets of water all over the Princess.

"She's wet!" shouted the children in the audience. "That's real water, isn't it?"

It *was* real water, and so Princess Ninetta was saved.

"Ssh!" said their parents. "Here comes Fata Morgana."

The Wicked Witch and Assistant Baddie Smeraldina crept out from behind the cardboard rock. The whole audience hissed and booed.

"Quick!" said Fata Morgana. "The King and his court are coming. Smeraldina, you pretend to be the Princess, and I shall work some magic on the real Princess Ninetta."

The Assistant Baddie pranced about in the Princess's crown, and Fata Morgana dragged Ninetta away, but returned almost at once holding hands with a rat who was wearing Ninetta's clothes.

"Ooh!" squeaked the children. "Poor Princess Ninetta! She's been magicked into a rat! Whatever will happen now?"

"Fata Morgana," said Pantaloon, "will take the Princess Rat to the infernal regions, and Assistant Baddie Smeraldina will pretend to be a princess. Listen to what she says to the King!"

"Are you the Princess Ninetta?" asked the King.

"Oh yes," said Smeraldina.

"No, no," cried the Prince. "She's much too ugly! This is not my beloved."

"That's not the real Princess!" all the children shouted out. "That's an assistant baddie!"

The King didn't seem to hear them. He said:

"It's true that she doesn't look particularly lovable, but still, you *did* say you would marry her and we can't have princes breaking their promises. Marry her you must. Bring her along, and let us return to the palace."

Assistant Baddie Smeraldina smirked, and the Prince began to look sad again. He dragged his feet and moaned quietly as the royal procession left the stage.

"Now, ladies and gentlemen," said Pantaloon, "our play is nearly over. Pompous Prime Minister is busy arranging the Prince's

wedding and in the infernal regions, Bad Witch Fata Morgana and Good Wizard Chelio are *still* quarrelling!"

"We're bored with Fata Morgana," cried a gang of young men in the audience. "She's stopping this story from having a happy ending."

They jumped on to the stage, grabbed the witch and took her away.

"Go on, Wizard!" they said. "Go and wave your magic wand and make a happy ending!"

Pantaloon stepped forward.

"This happy ending is a bit of a muddle … look at the throne. Can you see a giant rat sitting on it? That's poor Ninetta. Nasty Niece and Pompous Prime Minister are delighted. They think any King who allows rats to sit on his throne is clearly mad, and they will be asked to be King and Queen instead … but look! Good Wizard Chelio is coming to the rescue. He's throwing a magical silver cloth over the rat, and underneath … it's the beautiful Real Princess after all. What a relief!"

"Aah!" sighed the ladies happily in the audience. "True love triumphs after all!"

"Is *this* the young lady you fell in love with?" the King asked his son, pointing at Ninetta.

"Yes," said the Prince. "Oh, my darling, let us be married at once!"

"Indeed," said the King, "it is definitely time for a happy ending."

Musicians began to play, and the whole company of actors paraded round the stage. Even Fata Morgana was allowed to come back. The applause was deafening.

As the performers took their bows, Pantaloon sang a little song which went like this:

"Oranges have come and gone,
A princess hidden in each one.
The goodies have won,
The baddies are beaten,
A huge wedding-cake
Is about to be eaten.

So thank you for watching
And come again soon!
Goodbye and good luck
From your friend Pantaloon."

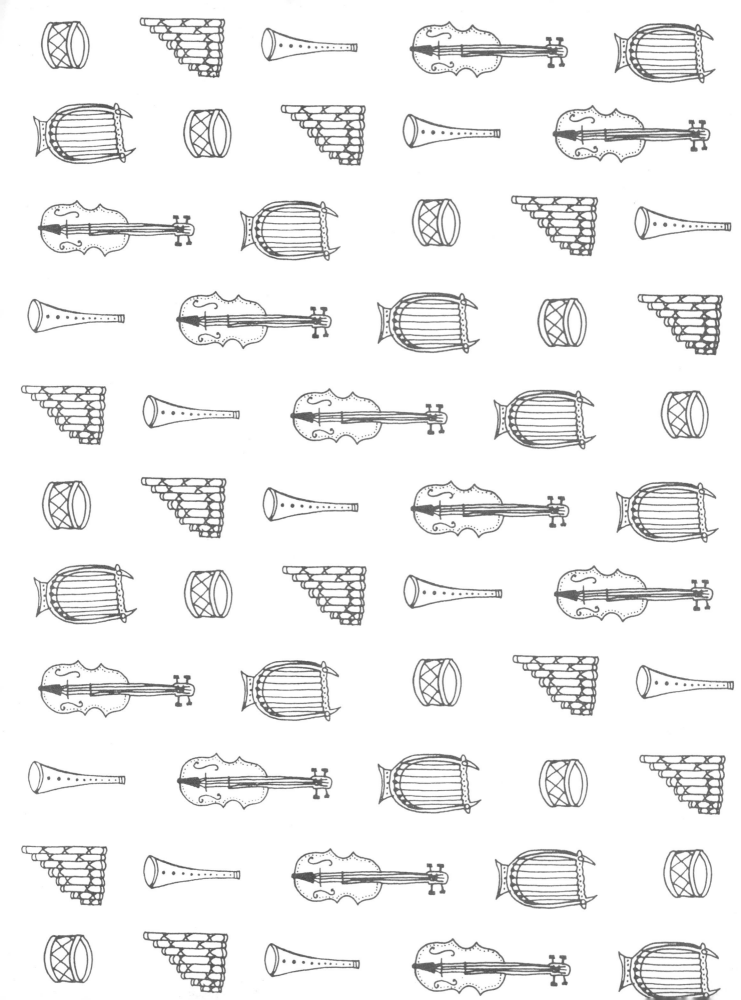